Baliem Ballet

One Girl's Quest for the Rest of the Story

J. David Scherling

InspiringVoices®
A Service of **Guideposts**

Inspiring Voices books may be ordered through booksellers or by contacting:

Inspiring Voices
1663 Liberty Drive
Bloomington, IN 47403
www.inspiringvoices.com
1-(866) 697-5313

ISBN: 978-1-4624-0428-5 (e)
ISBN: 978-1-4624-0427-8 (sc)
Library of Congress Control Number: 2012922169

Because of the dynamic nature of the Internet, any web addresses or links contained in this book may have changed since publication and may no longer be valid. The views expressed in this work are solely those of the author and do not necessarily reflect the views of the publisher, and the publisher hereby disclaims any responsibility for them.

Any people depicted in stock imagery provided by Thinkstock are models, and such images are being used for illustrative purposes only.
Certain stock imagery © Thinkstock.

Chapter 4
Quote taken from *Our Daily Bread*, 2009 by RBC Ministries, Grand Rapids, Michigan, and used by permission. All rights reserved.

Chapter 5
Adaptation from *DeShazer* by C.H. Watson, Seattle Pacific University, used by permission

Chapters 6 and 11
Lyrics of "I've Got a River of Life" are public domain

Chapter 6
Quote of limerick by Elizabeth Johnson, used by permission

Chapter 7
Quote from *Sketches of his Presence* by J. David Scherling, used by permission

Chapter 8
Quote from www.findadig.com, used by permission

All other quoted or referenced material is used by permission.

Unless otherwise noted, scripture taken from the New King James Version. Copyright 1979, 1980, 1982 by Thomas Nelson, inc. Used by permission. All rights reserved.

Printed in the United States of America
Inspiring Voices rev. date: 12/4/2012

For Delores

Preface

The Baliem River dances its way through the tropical island of Papua, Indonesia. Its headwaters, high in the mountains—some snow-capped peaks higher than sixteen thousand feet—are fed by melting snow and artesian springs. Dancing the reel, the Baliem River passes through highland villages of aboriginal peoples who, although they share similar cultures, speak many different languages. Reaching the central high valley area near Wamena, the Baliem tangoes through ever-ripening fields of fruits and vegetables and around the city of Wamena, which serves as the government, commercial, and aviation center of Papua. The few roads in the high valley extend only a short distance in each direction. The Baliem then jitterbugs through the deep and rocky gorges, collecting flow from several tributaries, to the flat lowland jungle on the south of Papua. Finally, weaving and turning, it quietly waltzes to the coast. Through the lowland it becomes a highway for boats, barges, and canoes, serving the villages along its banks. The Baliem truly is a river of life for many in Papua.

A ballet tells a story. The Baliem River has thousands, maybe millions, of stories. Here is one.

Acknowledgements

Baliem Ballet: One Girl's Quest for the Rest of the Story is a historical novel—a work of fiction. The basis for the story came to me while I was studying Isaiah 61:1–2, Luke 4:18–19, and Luke 7:22–23. Some of the incidents detailed in this book actually happened and are experiences I have thought about for years. Others occurred to me as the book came together.

Many places, people, and incidents are real and genuine. I have been there, know the people, and have seen the places, but in the book the names of people and some places have been changed (except in the case of well-known individuals) since it is a work of fiction. If anyone described is offended, I apologize and plead for forgiveness. Other places and people I invented to fit the situation.

I owe much gratitude to granddaughter Elizabeth Johnson, who wrote the journal entries from her own experience at school, and niece Kathryn McCannell, who actually participated in the 2009 archeological dig at Clunia, Spain, and found skeletal remains as described in her journal entries adapted in the book. Also to her dad, Daryle McCannell, a university professor, who invented the game "Pebble Toss" that John the Baptist's disciples played in the story.

I especially appreciate the help and encouragement of my wife, Delores, who proofread every line over and over and added so much to the story. Others who offered excellent comments are Jane Ardelean, Dow Chamberlain, Hattie Caswell, Valerie Johnson, Mary Jorud, Barbara Kroeker, Joyce Conkling, and Marie Gunderson.

Some writers of historical novels have been accused of devaluating or even revising the sacred Scriptures, changing traditional interpretations or meanings. I understand that I risk this possibility. It is not my intention to "add to Scripture" or devalue Scripture. My hope is that the Scriptures are always considered God's authoritative Word and divine revelation.

Chapter 1

Papuan Village—Spring, 1995

"Mommy, why do I have to wear this new dress? It scratches me!" Deena complained.

"It's so cute and makes you look like a little ballerina," her mother soothed. "You remember the story we watched where the actors danced while music played their parts? Weren't those girls pretty? Besides, your father has returned to the village and is coming to dinner, along with the pastor and his wife, and we want to let him see how beautiful you are and how well you are doing. You remember that your father loved your mother and after she died has not taken another wife. He loves you just as much."

"Mommy, why did God let my mother die and let me live?"

"We do not know yet, Deena, but maybe He has something special for you to do."

South Papuan Jungle—Spring, 1990

Lightning flashed. Thunder rolled. "The spirits must be mad at me again," Darius mused out loud to himself. *Why does it have to rain with such turbulent furor during the time of the full moon?*

Thunderstorms are a common relief to the hot, sunny days

1

in the swampy jungle of the southern Papuan lowlands. It rains almost every day but not always with scary thunder and lightning, which rarely continues after dark.

Darius thought of the foreign missionaries in the village. *Aylea and Carol tell us that God loves us, but I still think the spirits are out to get me. But then, I am also going against the advice of the village elders, hunting and gathering so far away. It would take us almost four days to get back to the village if something life-threatening happened here.*

"You better hurry and find some more palm fronds for the lean-to shelter you put up. The kids are getting wet, and I think the baby is coming," Darius's wife, Yolana, chided over the noise of the wind and rain, between thunderclaps.

She is so beautiful—tall and slender, still a teenager—yet expecting her third baby, he thought. Ana and Jorus are still very small and dependent. Why have I taken them so far from their grandparents and the help we need? I wonder if our ancestors who lived in the tree houses ever went through all this anxiety?

Frantically Darius searched for more fronds low enough to be cut in a hurry. Just then lightning bolted across the sky and brightened the area. He was able to see some fronds and hurried to hack them off with his machete. *This storm will bring out the snakes and leeches; we need to see them when they come. We also need to find some more dry wood for the fire.*

The swampy lowlands of South Papua are home to many native people groups who speak 268 different languages, according to the *Ethnologue*. They speak different languages but have a similar culture trait, what anthropologists generally call "cargo cult," meaning that they are forever expecting the spirits to provide them with great riches, inaugurating a period of prosperity. The people have similar aboriginal features, are dark-skinned with kinky hair, and wear similar clothing—grass skirts for the women and gourds for the men—and these groups are traditional enemies. Only in recent years have families dared to attempt to survive alone in the jungle as they hunt and gather for their subsistence. Fear of their enemies, natural disasters (storms, floods, fire), and illnesses haunt the people continually. They are plagued by malaria, elephantiasis (both transmitted by mosquitoes), malnutrition, infections, and other diseases; little hope of medical assistance exists. Wild beasts in the jungle, such as snakes, wild boars, cassowaries, crocodiles, poisonous insects, lizards, and huge bats with wingspans of three feet or more, can turn on their predators and kill them when confronted. Fear of these adversaries turns to panic whenever the reality of danger threatens the people.

Generally life is quite ordinary and routine, with days of hunting for wild hogs and other game such as crocodiles, large rodents, birds, and, in the higher areas, rabbits. When a hunter is fortunate enough to run across wild game, he shoots it with bow and arrow or, in some cases, poison darts from his homemade blow gun. Firearms and ammunition are not available to hunters in this area. While hunting, men and women look for wild and planted fruit and vegetable roots, such as breadfruit, bananas, papayas, palm berries, and sweet potatoes. Sago palm, a starchy staple, is also hunted for, but a group is preferred to harvest it. If a family intends to stay in a new area for a few months, they may clear a place in the jungle and plant some sweet potatoes for harvest before they return to the village.

I know the elders would rather that we live in the village, but do they somehow make the spirits mad at us and make hunting and gathering so difficult? Darius mused. *We are only here because the garden plots are all taken by other villagers, and the older ones are no longer fertile and therefore useless for gardens. Or is it that the spirits are so mad that they somehow keep the gardens from growing? No game to hunt, no fish to spear, no fruit or vegetables to gather, we have all had bouts of malaria, and now this weather, just when the baby is coming; why are the spirits so mad at us?* Darius tied up palm branches as the rain pounded down even more.

"Can you help me find more dry wood for this fire so that we have light and a little warmth?" Yolana sobbed. "The pains are coming closer together now."

"Okay, I'll do my best." *She knows getting firewood is a woman's job, but she's in trouble now, and besides, there are no elders here to see me. I can do that here—but I wonder if it will make the spirits madder.*

"Lay the kids down on their mats, and cover them with something warm," his wife instructed. "There are two shirts hanging on that branch—ahhhiiiooouu! That hurts!"

Her mother or grandmother should be here to help her as midwife, but then again, she has been through this before. Darius was worried, nervously wringing his hands. "Your mat is ready if you want to lie or sit on it. I put leaves under it," he said. "I have another new mat available, and I am ready to help catch the baby, if you need me."

"Help me—the fire feels good. The kids are quiet, and the rain seems to have let up a little." Yolana managed to comment between contractions as she squatted onto her mat birthing bed.

In a little while, the baby arrived. "It's a little girl. She's lovely!" Darius exclaimed as he gently wrapped her in a cloth and gave her to his wife.

"Your name is Deena." Yolana kissed her tenderly.

The next morning the sky was still cloudy, but the rain had stopped. The ground was covered with water, making mud everywhere. Ana and Jorus were taking turns holding and loving Deena when suddenly Darius heard his son screaming.

"Daddy, help! There's a snake going right for Mommy! Help—help!"

"Quick! Take Deena and Ana, and run away as fast as you can!" Darius grabbed his machete and went for the snake, but it was too late; it had already bitten Yolana on the arm, and she was bleeding. With one stroke of the machete, Darius cut off the snake's head, but it still writhed ferociously. *How I wish I was in the village—Aylea and Carol could help her. All I know to do is to let the wound bleed.*

Yolana died the next day. Darius dug a shallow grave for his wife and tenderly placed her in it. Then he and his children started the long hike to the village. *How will I ever make it before Deena also dies? I should bury Deena with Yolana.* "Ana, bring Deena," Darius instructed. "I will bury her with her mother."

"No, Daddy, don't. I will carry her in my *noken*."

"Okay, Ana, I'll help you." *But what will the elders think if I arrive and Deena has died?*

After four grueling days on the trail, making camp before each nightfall, they arrived in the village. Darius immediately took Deena to the missionaries' solid, clean, and comfortable house, even though all the women of the village wanted to see and hold the baby. "Please, later, she's almost dying. Yolana died four days ago, and Deena has had only sips of water to drink."

Then, turning to the missionary, he said, "*Ibu* Aylea, can you help me? Do you have some milk for my new baby daughter, Deena?"

"We will do our best. I'll call for an airplane flight right now and see if a doctor in the city can help us."

Miraculously, a mission airplane and pilot were available, and within two hours, the plane arrived to pick up Aylea and Deena. An hour later they were met at the airport by the doctor with infant formula and dehydration fluid. It wasn't until a week later that everyone had confidence Deena would live.

But all of the villagers wondered what would happen to her. *Darius can't possibly keep her; he has no milk and has to care for the other two children.*

Papuan Village—Spring, 1990

When Darius first arrived with Deena at the missionaries' house in the village, he found only Aylea Fuchida, the one from Japan, because Carol Penner, the one from America, was back in the city for a conference. Darius was just glad someone was there to help him. "Will you take care of Deena and keep her as your own baby daughter? I cannot take care of her in the jungle, and I want her to grow up to be just like you."

This, of course, was not an easy question, because although Aylea was already in love with Deena, she needed the permission of her mission as well as the backing of her family and her home church. Nevertheless, Aylea began the paperwork—the red tape—by registering her as Deena Charis Fuchida.

Papuan Village—Spring, 1995

By the time Darius returned again for the dinner when Deena wore her ballerina dress, she was already five years old. She enjoyed being homeschooled in preschool subjects, mainly number and letter recognition, and the opportunity to learn and love stories from the Bible.

"Deena," Darius exclaimed, "you are beautiful! You look just like your mother!"

Chapter 2

Papuan Village—Spring, 1998

"Mommy, tell me my favorite Bible story again!"

"Which one is that, dear—the one about Queen Esther, or the one about King David's grandmother, Ruth, or the one about Noah's ark?"

"No, Mommy, the one about John the Baptist."

"Okay. John the Baptist was born in a miraculous way," Aylea began. "Both his parents, Zacharias and Elizabeth, were from priestly heritage. You remember; this means their parents were priests, and thus, Zacharias also served as priest. They were very old and never had any children. One day Zacharias was fulfilling his annual duty, burning incense to the Lord in the temple, and the people outside were praying. Suddenly, an angel appeared to him, frightening him. The angel spoke: 'Fear not, Zacharias, for your prayers have been answered! Elizabeth will have a baby boy, and you will name him John. He will make you and many others very happy because he will be great in the eyes of the Lord. He must never touch wine or hard liquor. He will be filled with the Holy Spirit from before his birth. He will persuade many to return to the Lord. He will be a man of rugged spirit like Elijah, and he will prepare the way for the coming of the Messiah.'

"'Impossible,' Zacharias retorted. 'Both Elizabeth and I are too old to have children!'

"'I am Gabriel,' the angel said. 'God himself has sent me with this good news. Now, because of your unbelief, you will not be able to speak until this is all fulfilled. God will surely do what He says!'

"The people outside praying could not understand what was taking so long, and some thought Zacharias had died or hurt himself. When he finally came out, he could not speak, but only gestured. He fulfilled his duty at the temple in the next few weeks and then went home. Elizabeth was thrilled and praised the Lord when she found out she was pregnant.

"When John was born, all their friends rejoiced with them, and at the circumcision celebration expected the boy to be named Zacharias. But Elizabeth said, 'No, his name is John.' When they asked Zacharias what the baby's name was, he asked for a writing tablet and wrote: *His name is John!* At that moment, Zacharias was able to speak again and praised the Lord. The Bible says John grew up in the wilderness and grew in his relationship with God and his knowledge of God."

Deena interrupted, "That's one of the parts of the story I really like!"

"Why is that, Deena?"

"Because John the Baptist grew up in the wilderness just like me and my friends." And then, changing the subject, Deena asked, "Mommy, the boys are getting ready to play soccer. May I go out and play with them?"

"Of course, sweetheart. Girls can play soccer, as well as be ballerinas, but be careful, and don't hurt yourself."

"Mommy, do you think John the Baptist and his disciples ever played soccer?"

She was gone before Aylea had a chance to answer. But the question was haunting. *Wouldn't it be neat if we knew exactly what happened—all the details of the stories in Scripture?*

East Bank Wilderness Camp—Spring, AD 27

"It's your turn, Lemuel. If you get this one, the game's over!"

"What are you guys doing?" They were startled by the question and looked up to see a stranger with a sword. His accent gave him away as a Judean, but the ridiculous question made him seem like a foreigner.

"What's this—were you just born yesterday? Haven't you ever played Pebble Toss?"

"Pebble Toss? Never heard of it. How does it go?"

"It's a game for two or more guys. We all sit in a circle or across from each other. So if you have more than, maybe, twelve, the circle gets too large. In the middle of the circle, or between the two of us, we have what we call a stick pouch." Lemuel showed the stranger a piece of lambskin about two hands across in both directions—about one cubit by one cubit—draped over three sticks that were each about one cubit in height stuck into the ground. "The skin is draped and tied in such a way to the tops of the three sticks, like this, so that a small pocket is formed. We sit around taking turns throwing small pebbles, trying to get the pebble to land in and stay in the pocket."

"Sounds like fun—or at least, something to while away the time. Is that all there is to it?"

"No, there's more; let's see if I can remember the rules we use. First, we all choose ten small pebbles that are approximately the same size—about the size of the end of your finger. Then, we also choose two small pebbles called 'freedom stones' that are the same color, but a different color from the other ten. What else, Josueh?"

"Well, to start, we each toss a pebble at the stick pouch trying to get it to stay in the pocket. The player whose pebble stays in the pouch begins the game. If more than one stays in the pouch after the first round, those players continue until only one stays in the pouch, and he begins. Then the first person throws his pebble, and around the circle we go.

"If he makes a 'pouch,' or sometimes we call it a 'basket-pocket,' he can take a chance and take a toss with one of his freedom stones. If he also gets his freedom stone in the pouch, he can claim all the pebbles that are in the pouch. If he misses, he has to give up one of his regular pebbles by placing it in the pouch—along with the freedom stone that he tossed and missed.

"Next, players can choose to toss their freedom stones at any time to claim the pouch. But they could also lose their freedom stone and one other of their pebbles. The winner is the one who ends up with the most stones. You get one point for regular pebbles and two points for each freedom stone. The game ends after twelve rounds," Josueh concluded.

"By the way, what are you doing here?" Lemuel asked the stranger.

"I came to see the rabbi. The one called John the Baptizer."

"You need to talk to Andrew. That's him right over there."

"Rabbi, there's a young man here to see you—I think he wants to join our circle."

Rabbi John the Baptizer, as he was affectionately called, turned and stroked his long, shaggy beard. "What do you think, Andrew, is there room for another disciple in our camp?"

"My feeling is that there is always room for one more of the right persuasion, but this one seems rather zealous, or maybe politically ambitious," Andrew replied quietly.

"What's his name?"

"Simon, from Judea."

"Not Simon the fisherman, from Galilee? I've heard about him!"

"No, no, not my brother. Simon Peter's a little obnoxious, for sure, but he can pull in fishing nets with the best of them."

"Show him in, Andrew."

Andrew returned with a short, wiry, clean-shaven, and very well-dressed young man in a long, clean, white-hooded robe and new leather sandals. The sword tied around his waist appeared extremely well cared for. John, on the other hand, dressed in the traditional camel's skin tunic and broad leather belt of the old time prophets, was tall—nearly four cubits—and hardened from years of wilderness living and eating only available food like locusts and wild honey. His uncut hair was tied with a leather thong at the nape of his neck. John stood as Simon was introduced.

"The peace of God be with you, Simon. Andrew tells me you are asking about the possibility of joining our band. What makes you want to leave the sacred halls of Jerusalem and the many learned doctors of the Law to come here and be taught in this wilderness?"

"Rabbi, you are highly admired and talked about everywhere."

"Really, Simon? What do you mean—and in what ways?"

"To begin with, both your parents were from priestly families. And your birth was somewhat unusual, almost miraculous. Your background with the Essenes goes far beyond the usual 'run-of-the-rabbi' training in Jerusalem. But more than that, Rabbi, your teaching is said to be radical, even to the extent that you claim to be preparing the country for the coming of the Messiah. I am very interested in hastening the day of the Lord, as the prophets say."

"I see," pondered John, stroking his beard again. "Tell me, Simon, do you think that day is near?"

"Everyone in Jerusalem is talking about it. We are entering the four hundred and eighty-third year since King Cyrus of Persia gave the order to rebuild the temple. This is the year prophesied that the Messiah would enter it."

"That's right! Daniel, quoting the angel Gabriel, wrote, 'Know therefore and understand, that from the going forth of the command to restore the Temple and build Jerusalem until Messiah the Prince, there shall be seven sevens and sixty-two sevens,' which makes a total of 483 years." John paused. "You say everyone is talking about it?"

"Yes, especially those really concerned—the Pharisees, priests, and Levites."

"On another subject, Simon, are you sure you are ready? Can you drink the cup that we drink?"

"What do you mean?" *Can't he see I have my sword?*

"As you know, I have been a Nazarite since birth; we do not participate in worldly activities or eat rich, fattened foods. We dress unembellished and survive on what God provides."

"But your disciples are not Nazarites?"

"No, and as a learner with me, you do not have to be as strict in eating and dressing as I am, but austere living and godly character are part of the training here. And, what about you, Simon? What are your goals and ambitions?"

"As a lad, my goal was always to join the freedom fighters of Barabbas, but since his imprisonment and the subsequent breakup of the company, I have been looking for another mission. My uncle, a prominent businessman, encouraged me to look you up."

Standing and again stroking his beard, John called, "Andrew, I think Simon the Zealot, will give us a go. Please show him where he can roll out his mat."

As the two walked away, Simon wondered out loud, "This outfit that John wears, what's that all about?"

"You remember that Elijah and some of the other ancient prophets wore this stark and rustic uniform? Some of the Essene community do also, feeling that this austerity may help keep their minds focused on the Lord rather than on the things of the world. Personally, I think John has the spirit of Elijah, spoken of by the prophet, who will appear prior to the coming of the Messiah, even though John himself denies it."

"Why would John want to deny it?"

"Probably because Elijah did not die, but was taken up by a chariot and a whirlwind and many Pharisees think that he will return physically. John knows that he is not that Elijah. Also, many teachers interpret those prophecies as part of the final judgment and *not* referring to the coming of the Messiah."

Arriving at the cave, Andrew continued the orientation, "Here you go, Simon. You can stake your claim to this area next to disciples Lemuel and Josueh in the back of the cave. Your sword should be safe here if you hide it under your mat. I think John will want us to be on our way to the Jordan River now because people are no doubt already waiting for him there."

"Sounds good, Andrew, and I will hide my sword this time, but if it ever is needed, I won't hesitate to use it."

As they made their way out of the cave, Lemuel and Josueh were preparing the camp for their departure. "What is Lemuel doing to the fire?" asked Simon.

Andrew explained that he was covering the fire with a big flat stone to dampen the flame so it would keep burning slowly while they were away but also keep the fire from being seen from the outside.

As John and his disciples wound their way down the mountainside through a maze of huge rocks and boulders, thus concealing the entrance to their camp, he began the teaching session. "For Simon's benefit, I want to remind you that we have been discussing Isaiah's prophecies concerning the coming of the Messiah. We all know that the Messiah is coming to reestablish the Davidic throne and kingdom, but Isaiah also prophesies that He will suffer and die. Isaiah compares Him to a sacrificial lamb, possibly referring to the Passover Lamb or lamb of atonement as described in the Torah:

> 'He was despised, and we did not esteem Him.
> Surely He has borne our griefs
> And carried our sorrows;
> Yet we esteemed Him stricken,
> Smitten by God, and afflicted.
> But He was wounded for our transgressions,
> He was bruised for our iniquities;

The chastisement for our peace was upon Him,
And by His stripes we are healed.
All we like sheep have gone astray;
We have turned, every one, to his own way;
And the Lord has laid on Him the iniquity of us all.
He was oppressed and He was afflicted,
Yet He opened not His mouth;
He was led as a lamb to the slaughter,
And as a sheep before its shearers is silent,
So He opened not His mouth.'"

"Rabbi, how do you know that?"

"Thank you, Simon, for asking. As you know, since Scripture copies in the synagogues are well-guarded, to have a chance to read the prophet Isaiah for yourself is a rare occasion. So generally, you must make the most of every opportunity to read it yourself as well as when you hear it from others who know it. At the Essene commune, there is a copy of Isaiah's prophecy that I was given the privilege to read and study. With deep appreciation, I memorized several passages and made notes of others, especially about who the Messiah is and what he will do. This portion I just quoted tells us that the Messiah is God's sacrificial Lamb for the sins of the world.

"Isaiah also wrote:

'Seek the Lord while He may be found,
Call upon Him while He is near.
Let the wicked forsake his way,
And the unrighteous man his thoughts;
Let him return to the Lord,
And He will have mercy on him;

And to our God,
For He will abundantly pardon.'

"God has given me the specific assignment to call the people to repentance and baptize them as their commitment to serve God in holiness," John continued. "Another prophet also said:

'For I am the Lord, I do not change;
Therefore you are not consumed, O sons of Jacob.
Yet from the days of your fathers
You have gone away from My ordinances
And have not kept them.
Return to Me, and I will return to you,"
Says the Lord of hosts.'"

"Rabbi, I think I understand the need for repentance, but what is the importance of baptism? I don't remember baptism being taught in the Law and the prophets."

"Good question, Simon. As you know, the Law provides for purification and ceremonial washing, and we Jews are more exacting on that point than other peoples, because it is what God wants. The baptism of repentance we do is not new, however. The Essenes have been performing the ritual for nearly a century, but I do it because God has told me specifically to do this as a demonstration of the people's repentance and commitment to live holy lives. Further, God has instructed me to tell the people that I baptize with water, but the Messiah will do a new thing: He will baptize with the Holy Spirit and with fire." John paused. "Simon, we are almost to the river. If you would like to repent and be baptized, you may be the first today."

"Yes, I would, Rabbi."

Papuan Village—Spring, 1998

"Mommy, you said that here, in Luke 4, Jesus is reading from Isaiah 61. Did John the Baptist know about the old, old book of Isaiah?"

"I think that John the Baptist, even though he grew up in the wilderness, had a good teacher who taught him about Old Testament history and prophecies. Wouldn't it be neat if we knew everything that happened?"

East Bank Wilderness Camp—Spring, AD 27

The next morning, as the small band of learners prepared to go back down to the river, Simon indicated he would like to say something.

"Rabbi, may I say how much I appreciate your kind invitation to join your disciples? Since the nickname you have christened me with may stick, I would also like to say that I am no longer a Zealot in the political sense but a zealot for the Messiah. Please help me to stay focused on Him."

"Of course, Simon. We will expect you to also help us all maintain this high level of devotion to God and His Messiah." John faced the group. "Today we want to continue our discussion about what this Messiah will do. I believe God is vitally interested in the spiritual revival and restoration of His chosen people, as well as other people from all nations, to the devotion He desires. However, Isaiah also describes the Messiah as one who leads the people in social action. Men, can you remember some of the activities Isaiah mentions that the Messiah will do for the people?"

"What about feeding the poor and hungry?"

"Thank you. God is very concerned about the poor and the hungry and often chides his people for not caring enough, even through the prophet Isaiah. But amazingly, I cannot find any place where Isaiah said the Messiah would feed the hungry. He will preach the good news of hope and salvation to the poor and promises restoration, but feeding appears to be something that we as His people should be doing. According to Isaiah, the Messiah will do things we normally cannot do."

"Maybe like healing the sick?"

"Yes! In several places Isaiah mentions the Messiah will heal the sick. For example, Isaiah says, *The blind will see, the deaf will hear, the lame will walk, and even the dead will be brought back to life.* Is there anything else we can expect the Messiah will do?"

"In the Psalms we read that the Messiah will free the prisoners. Does Isaiah mention this as well?"

"Yes, at least three times Isaiah writes that the Messiah will set the captives free and provide liberty to the prisoners. That is why we can so boldly condemn the sins of the people today, as we preach repentance, because when the Messiah comes, He will set the prisoners free."

As they approached the river and the crowds waiting there, John motioned to his disciples to help the people get ready for his preaching and their baptisms.

Wading out into the river to a point about knee deep, John shouted out to the people, "Men of Israel, I am the one spoken of by the prophet when he said,

19

'The voice of one crying in the wilderness:
Prepare the way of the Lord;
Make straight in the desert
A highway for our God.
Every valley shall be exalted
And every mountain and hill brought low;
The crooked places shall be made straight
And the rough places smooth;
The glory of the Lord shall be revealed,
And all flesh shall see it together;
For the mouth of the Lord has spoken.'"

Someone shouted the words that were in the hearts of many: "What did the prophet mean by the words 'prepare the way of the Lord?'"

"To prepare yourselves for the coming of the Messiah, you must repent, turn from your wicked and selfish ways, and return to devotion and worship of the Lord your God," John replied. "You generation of vipers, who has warned you to flee from God's wrath to come? Repent and make sure your lives bear the good fruit that proves your sincerity. Do not rationalize to yourselves, thinking, 'We have Abraham as *our* father.' I tell you, God is able to make these stones to become children of Abraham. With his axe in his hand, the husbandman, scrutinizing his vineyard, is preparing to chop down every tree not bearing good fruit, and cast it into the fire."

Moved with conviction, some of those in the crowd wondered aloud, "What shall we do then?"

"Repent and be baptized as a demonstration of your commitment to live dedicated and holy lives. But more than that—you, who have two coats, share one with someone who has none; and those who have food, likewise share your provisions with the poor and hungry."

To the tax collectors notorious for their corruption, who also came to repent and be baptized, he admonished, "Charge no more than that which is required."

Soldiers in the crowd also pled for clarification, and he warned them, "Do violence to no one nor accuse anyone falsely, and be content with your wages."

On the way back to camp, Simon walked with Andrew. "I'm going to get my sword and sell it this evening. There were several poor people at the river today who could use some help."

The group walked a few more steps and Andrew cried, "Good for you, Simon. God will provide! Something is bothering me also. Rabbi, what does the prophet mean when he said, 'all flesh shall see the salvation of God?'"

"Good question, Andrew. God chose the children of Israel to be His representatives on earth. Their success and worship of God was to be a light and a witness so that the other nations could not resist the desire to know and worship Him also. As you know, our people strayed from God, and because of our sin, other nations oppose us and our God. Isaiah, in several prophecies about the Messiah, indicates that God is sending Him to do what we have failed to do—that is, convince them they need to come to Him also."

———

A few days later, sensing some apprehension among his small band of disciples, John opened the training session with a question: "Brothers, do you have any concerns or questions regarding what we have been discussing on the training walks or in the preaching times?"

One man spoke up. "Rabbi, we have been hearing more and more comments from the people in the crowds about the possibility that you, yourself, are the Messiah. How should we respond?"

"Thanks for that question, Andrew. I, too, have been sensing this desperate feeling among the people. When they repent and turn to God, experiencing forgiveness, they tend to think God's power is in the messenger. But you men know for sure that this is not the case. God is sending His Messiah, who is preferred before me, because He was before me. He is the Creator of the world and of His fullness we all have received, and grace upon grace. As you know, the Law was given by Moses, but grace and truth will come by the Christ. No one has seen God at any time, but God's only Son, the Messiah, sent from the heart of the Father, has seen Him and will represent Him. Tell the people that God has revealed to me, merely God's special messenger, that the Messiah will appear soon."

At the river, priests and Levites, dressed in their ecclesiastical garb and sent from the Jewish leaders in Jerusalem, approached John. "Who are you, really?" they asked.

"I am not the Christ!" John confessed, emphatically.

"Well, what then? Are you Elijah?"

"No, I am not Elijah."

"Do you mean to say that you are not that prophet?"

John responded politely, "No, I am not that prophet."

Unnerved, they continued grilling him one after another: "Who are you, then?"

"We need an answer to give to the leaders who sent us."

"What do you say of yourself?"

John patiently explained to the priests and Levites sent by Pharisees, who should have known already, "*I am the voice of one crying in the wilderness. Make straight the way of the Lord,* as said the prophet Isaiah."

Needing more, they persisted, "Why do you baptize, then, if you are not the Messiah, or even Elijah?"

"I indeed baptize you with water unto repentance. But He that comes after me is mightier than I, whose shoes I am not worthy to bear or even unloose. He shall baptize you with the Holy Ghost and with fire. His fan is in His hand, and He will thoroughly purge His floor, and gather His wheat into the garner, but He will burn up the chaff with unquenchable fire."

On the way back to the camp, Simon chatted with Andrew. "What did John mean when he told the priests that 'the Messiah would gather His wheat into His garner and burn up the chaff?'"

"Jewish religious leaders have deceived the people for years by making up their own traditions and leaving God out of their hearts and their lives. John was warning them to repent and return to the Lord and become, again, good wheat, and not chaff that will be burned. You remember that Jonah preached 'hellfire and brimstone' to the people of Nineveh, and they repented. John is hoping that these leaders will remember that and also repent before it is too late."

Chapter 3

Papuan Village—Spring, 1998

"Mommy, I thought Jesus never did anything wrong. Why did Jesus have to be baptized by John the Baptist?"

"Well, I can't say for sure, but it was partly to fulfill prophecy, but also to show support for what John was doing. I also think that Jesus was ready to submit to whatever was required of Him, even though He was God and did not need salvation or even repentance. What do you think?"

"Maybe He wanted to meet His cousin and find out what God would do for all the people there."

"That is no doubt true as well. Wouldn't it be nice if the Scriptures explained all that for us?"

East Bank Wilderness Camp—Spring, AD 27

The next day John worked hard counseling and baptizing the huge crowd that waited to be baptized. Near the end of the afternoon he saw Jesus coming toward him and shouted to the crowd, "Attention, everyone! Look over here! Behold! The Lamb of God who takes away the sin of the world! This is He of whom I said, 'After me comes a Man who is preferred before me, for He was before me. The one whose shoes I am unworthy to loose or carry.'"

Then to Jesus, trying to dissuade Him, he said softly, "I need to be baptized by you. And are you coming to me?"

But Jesus answered, "Please allow it to be done now, because it is proper for us to fulfill all righteousness."

"As you wish." When Jesus had been baptized, He came up immediately from the water, and there up in the sky, the heavens were opened to Him. John saw the Spirit of God descending like a dove and alighting upon Him. And suddenly a voice came from heaven, saying, "This is my beloved Son, in whom I am well pleased."

John the Baptist dismissed the crowd. "You have just experienced a momentous event, possibly the most significant of your lifetimes! Please return to your homes, and reflect on what this means for your families and for the world. You may return for more ministry in the morning."

Unable to contain their curiosity, the disciples began to ask John about the event. "How did you know it was Him?"

"When I was a little boy, my mother told me that this distant cousin of mine was a very special individual sent from God in a miraculous way. We have been expecting Him to do great things, but He seemed very ordinary as far as I knew—He lived way up there in Galilee. I did not know who the Messiah would be, but when I saw Him, the Holy Spirit said, 'This is the One.' And when God sent me to baptize with water, He said to me, 'Upon whom you see the Spirit descending and remaining on Him, this is He who baptizes with the Holy Spirit.' And I have seen and now testify that this is the Son of God."

"The Messiah has come! The Messiah has come! The Messiah

has come!" They could not stop repeating this news to one another. Finally, Andrew dared to approach John with a question on his heart.

"Rabbi, if Jesus, the Messiah of God, comes by here again, would you approve if He were willing to accept me as His disciple?"

"I would hate to see you leave, Andrew, but I must decrease, and He must increase. If that seems right to you in God's eyes, you certainly have my approval and blessing."

The next day, as John was with his disciples preaching and baptizing, Jesus again came to the river.

"There He is again—the Lamb of God who takes away the sin of the world."

Seeing Jesus, Andrew looked excitedly at Simon. "Let's check Him out to see if He is the Messiah and if we can join Him for training."

"Yeah, let's give it a try; John said it would be all right." Then, turning to question John, just to double-check, they saw John nodding his agreement.

Andrew and Simon, leaving their belongings in the camp-cave, began to follow after Jesus as He walked away. Soon Jesus turned and asked, "What do you want? Can I help you with something?"

"Rabbi, where are you staying?" Andrew and Simon, in unison, asked the traditional question that learners used to request acceptance.

"Come and see." So Andrew the Galilean and Simon the Zealot left John the Baptizer and became two of the first disciples of Jesus the Messiah.

Papuan Village—Spring, 1998

"Mommy, did John the Baptist baptize any other important people besides Jesus?" Deena questioned after reading, again, the story in her Bible story book.

"Well, the Scriptures do not record any actual baptisms of prominent people, but in Acts, some people were converted who only knew John's baptism. One of them I would call prominent, and it could be that he was baptized by John, even though he was from North Africa. His name was Apollos."

East Bank Wilderness Camp—Spring, AD 27

Left with just two disciples, John began to look for promising recruits. During the Passover week celebration, many Jewish adherents came from distant lands, and having heard about John's ministry, gathered at the Jordan River to see and experience the powerful challenge of John's message. One day that week, John noticed an extremely well-dressed and good-looking young man next in line for baptism and asked, "You are not from Judea, are you?"

"No. I'm from Alexandria—here for the Passover celebration—my first time in Judea."

"Why did you come to be baptized?"

"I am seeking all the information I can find on the Messiah promised in Scripture, and everyone says this is the place to be."

"If your heart is right, and you follow God's leading and His Word, He will not disappoint you. What is your name?"

"Apollos."

"Are you Greek?"

"No, sir, I am Hebrew, of the Tribe of Simeon, born in Alexandria. God has blessed our family there."

"Are you looking for a rabbi to study under?"

"Not here, Rabbi. I am needed back in Alexandria, and Father is anxious that I study the Scriptures there. However, I could stay until the Feast of the Tabernacles, if that would be all right."

"We would love to have you with us. May God continue to bless your efforts."

"Rabbi, one more question, please: When I do return to Alexandria, may I use your methods to challenge the people in Africa to repent and prepare for the Messiah's coming?"

"I would be honored, Apollos, but be sure to pay close attention to the 'suffering servant' Messianic passages in the Psalms and Isaiah. And be prepared for severe persecution. We'll talk more about that in the next fifty days."

"*Shalom*, Rabbi."

Later, in the fall, when the Jordan had dried up to a trickle, John and his disciples crossed over to the west bank and north to Samaria. There they found a wilderness camp site near Aenon and baptized where there was plenty of water. Jesus and his disciples left Jerusalem, but they stayed in Judea and baptized there. People kept coming to John for baptism, but Jesus was baptizing near the area where John had left, and many were also coming to His disciples for baptism. About that time, a certain Jew began an argument with John's disciples over ceremonial cleansing.

"You know that your baptism does not meet the requirements of the Law for cleansing," he argued.

"The ceremonial cleansing of the Law does not clean your heart," Lemuel responded. "You need to repent and commit to serving the Lord in holiness."

"Jesus is baptizing more seekers than you are," he countered.

"Many people need to repent," Josueh conceded, but he and the other disciples began to wonder what was happening. So they went to John and asked, "Teacher, the man you met on the other side of the Jordan River, the one you said was the Messiah, is also baptizing people. Why is everybody going over there instead of coming here to us?"

"God in heaven appoints each person's work," John responded quietly. "You yourselves know how plainly I told you that I am not the Messiah. I am here to prepare the way for Him—that is all. The bride will go where the bridegroom is. A bridegroom's friend rejoices with him. I am the bridegroom's friend, and I am filled with joy at His success. He must become greater and greater, and I must become less and less.

"He has come from above and is greater than anyone else. I am of the earth, and my understanding is limited to the things of earth, but He has come from heaven. He tells what He has seen and heard, but how few believe what He tells them! Those who believe Him discover that God is true, because He is sent by God. He speaks God's words, for God's Spirit is upon Him without measure or limit. The Father loves His Son, and He has given Him authority over everything. And all who believe in God's Son have eternal life. Those who don't obey the Son will never experience eternal life, but the wrath of God remains upon them."

"Rabbi, you will never guess what happened last Sabbath Day in Galilee!" Lemuel exclaimed one evening as he bounded into camp, having just arrived from visiting his family in Galilee. With the coming of the winter rains, Jesus and His disciples had left Judea to minister in Galilee, while John and his disciples had also returned from Samaria to their east bank camp.

"Good to have you back, Lem. You ran into Jesus while you were there?"

"Not only did I see Him, but what He did was something you told us He would do!"

"What was that?"

"Well, the night before the Sabbath I found myself in Nazareth, Jesus' home town, while visiting my sister. She reminded me that I'd better not go further until after the Sabbath, so I stayed with her family. The next day, we all went to the synagogue, as usual, and Simon and Andrew were there with Jesus and some other disciples. It was good to see them, but the really exciting thing was the possibility of hearing Jesus speak. When He got up to speak, He asked for the scroll of the Prophet Isaiah, turned to the portion we have discussed, and read:

"The Spirit of the Lord is upon Me, because He has anointed Me to preach the gospel to the poor; He has sent Me to heal the brokenhearted, to proclaim liberty to the captives and recovery of sight to the blind, to set at liberty those who are oppressed; to proclaim the acceptable year of the Lord. Then He rerolled the scroll, gave it back to the attendant, and sat down to speak. He had everyone's attention—you could have heard a pin drop. Then He said, 'Today these Scriptures have been fulfilled in your hearing.' Simon, Andrew, and I all knew He was saying that He is the Messiah because you told us, but we think most everyone else did not understand."

Back at the river, John continued to condemn the sins of the people and invite them to repent and return to the Lord, using the words of the Prophet Isaiah.

"Is anyone thirsty? Come and drink—even if you have no money! Come, take your choice of wine or milk—it's all free! Why spend your money on food that does not give you strength? Why pay for food that does you no good? Listen and I will tell you where to get food that is good for the soul! Seek the Lord while you can find Him. Call on Him now while He is near. Turn from your wicked deeds. Banish from your minds the very thought of doing wrong! Turn to the Lord, and He may have mercy on you. Yes, turn to our God, for He will abundantly pardon.

"You generation of vipers, who has warned you to flee from God's wrath to come? Even your king, right here in Perea, is shocking all Israel with his sin—taking his brother's wife when both are still married—what a disgrace! Repent today, and make sure your lives bear the good fruit that proves your sincerity."

It did not take long for those words to reach the ears of King Herod and his new wife, Herodius. The next day as John was baptizing, Josueh observed, "Rabbi, the soldiers have returned."

Looking up, John admonished, "You soldiers have already been baptized, and do not need to repeat, unless the first was done for show, and this is for real."

"No, Rabbi, we are not here for baptism—the first was for real. The King has sent us with a personal invitation for you to come to his palace. He said to tell you that the leaders in Jerusalem are not happy with your ministry and are planning some reprisals. You and your disciples will be safe at the Machaerus Palace."

"Tell me—Sergeant Rufus, isn't it? What if we decided to return to Samaria and baptize there?"

"I will not be induced to do violence, but as you know, Rabbi, I must obey my orders."

"All right, men; let's go see how the aristocrats live."

The guest suite at the palace was very comfortable and well-appointed. But it soon became evident that John was a prisoner—the guard never left. John was free to teach his disciples, and the disciples were free to come and go as they wished, but John remained in the guest rooms. At first John thought that he would have the opportunity to personally share his feelings about the king's lifestyle, but neither Herod nor Herodius ever appeared. Whether they had returned to their Jerusalem quarters, or just did not want to be bothered, was not explained.

"Rabbi," Josueh ventured one day, after they had been at the palace a few weeks, "can we review what Isaiah said the Messiah would do?"

"But of course, Josie. What do you remember Isaiah saying?"

"What I remember is: 'The lame will walk, the blind will see, the deaf will hear, the prisoners will be set free, the dead will be raised, and the gospel will be preached to the poor.'"

"Very good! Do you remember anything else, Lem?"

"Not really, but here's what bothers us: If Jesus is the Messiah and is doing all those things, why are we still in prison?"

"Maybe He is not doing all those things."

"How can we find out?"

"Why don't you and Josueh plan a little field trip and go to Galilee and ask Him?"

"Do you really think we can do that?"

"Yes, I do. Sergeant Rufus, will you help Lemuel and Josueh gather the provisions needed for a field trip to Galilee?"

In Galilee, a few days later, Andrew shouted to Simon the Zealot. "Look! Here come Lem and Josueh!"

"Lem and Josie, what are you doing here?"

"Maybe you have heard that John is in prison at the Machaerus Palace. He requested that we come and ask Jesus a question. Can we do that now?"

"Jesus is quite busy with the crowds here, but let's go and watch, and when there is a break, we will introduce you."

The four of them made their way to the front of the crowd and watched as Jesus tenderly attended the sick. He was holding a little girl with two club feet. "Can you walk, sweetheart?"

"No, but I can crawl, and if someone holds my hand, I can take a few steps."

"Would you like to walk and run?"

"Oh yes! Please help me!"

Jesus carefully touched her feet, and as they watched, both feet and ankles straightened out. The little girl stood up and jumped and ran around the crowd, praising God. "Thank you, Jesus! Thank you, Jesus! Glory to God!"

Jesus nodded to the next in line, an old man.

"Master, I am blind, can you help me?"

"How long have you been like this?"

"I have been losing my sight for several years, but I've been completely blind for only a few months."

Jesus touched his eyes and asked, "Do you believe I am the Messiah, the Son of God?"

"Yes, you are the Son of God and can heal me!"

"Be healed!"

"Thank you, Master! I can see again! Praise God!"

"What is your name, son?" Jesus asked the next in line.

"His name is Daniel, but he cannot hear you. He has been deaf since birth."

"God has healed you, my son. Go in peace, and give Him the glory!"

Next in line was a very pretty young lady who appeared sullen and angry. With her was an older woman.

"And you, young lady, are not happy to be here. Are evil spirits antagonizing you?"

"My daughter is not herself these days. Can you help her?"

Jesus spoke directly to the offending demons: "Come out of her and return to the abyss." And then, to the girl, "How do you feel now, young lady?"

"Free and at peace. Praise be to God!"

"Rabbi?"

Jesus glanced up. "Thank you, Andrew. I need a break."

"Rabbi, two of John's disciples are here with greetings and a question from John. He is in prison at Machaerus Palace. This is Lemuel and Josueh."

"May God's peace be with you, Lem and Josie."

"God's peace be with You as well, Rabbi. John the Baptist sent us to ask: Are you the Messiah we've been expecting, or should we keep looking for someone else?"

"Go back to John and tell him what you have witnessed—the blind seeing, the lame walking, lepers cured, evil spirits cast out, the deaf hearing, the dead raised to life, and the Good News being preached to the poor. And tell him, 'God blesses those who are not offended by me.'"

Back at Machaerus Palace, Lemuel and Josueh repeated what Jesus had said. Lemuel added, "Jesus is fulfilling all Isaiah prophesied except the part about freeing the prisoners. Why is that?"

"Why did you not ask Him?"

"We wanted to, but He was so authoritative, and He rather put us in our place with the words, 'Blessed is he who does not doubt.'"

"You know, maybe Isaiah was referring to those who are captives and prisoners to sin and not those who are in a literal prison. But we will be blessed if we do not doubt Him."

A few weeks later, Andrew announced again that Lemuel and Josueh were arriving—this time in sackcloth and ashes, the traditional mourning attire. Jesus immediately stopped what He was doing and ran to them, embracing them. "Blessed are they that mourn, for they shall be comforted. "God's peace be with you," He said, and then quietly surmised, "John is dead. Tell us how it happened."

"King Herod was celebrating his birthday with a big party for all of those officials important to him. There was much liquor and carousing. Finally, he asked Salome, daughter of his brother Philip, to dance. He was so enthralled with her that he promised her whatever she wanted, even if it were half of his kingdom. Salome consulted her mother about what to ask for and she said, 'The head of John the Baptist on a platter.' Herod sent his soldiers to the room where John was held and beheaded him. We took his body and buried it."

Weeping, Jesus lauded, "John was more than a prophet. John was the man to whom the Scriptures refer when they say, 'Look, I am sending my messenger before you, and he will prepare your way before you.' I tell you, of all who have ever lived, none is greater than John. Yet even the most insignificant person in the Kingdom of God is greater than he is!" Finally, Jesus addressed the men before him.

"Lemuel and Josueh, please join our group of seventy. Lemuel will be called Lemuel Matthias and Josueh, Josueh Justus."

Papuan Village—Spring, 1998

"Mommy, why didn't Jesus free John the Baptist?"

"I don't know, Deena. But maybe someday we will know."

Chapter 4

Sentani, Papua—Christmas, 2000

"Deena, please read to me the passage from Luke's gospel that you will be reading in the Christmas program. I would like to hear how you pronounce all the words. *Quirinius* is kind of tough to pronounce."

"Okay, Mom, here goes. Luke 2, verses 1–7:

> 'And it came to pass in those days that a decree went out from Caesar Augustus that all the world should be registered. This census first took place while Quirinius was governing Syria. So all went to be registered everyone to his own city. Joseph also went up from Galilee, out of the city of Nazareth, into Judea, to the city of David, which is called Bethlehem, because he was of the house and lineage of David, to be registered with Mary, his betrothed wife, who was with child. So it was, that while they were there, the days were completed for her to be delivered. And she brought forth her firstborn Son, and wrapped Him in swaddling cloths, and laid Him in a manger, because there was no room for them in the inn.'"

"You did very well, Deena," Aylea beamed. "I'm sure everyone else will think so, too!"

"Mommy, why did God send Jesus to be born in a cattle shed and be given the cattle's feeding trough as a cradle?"

"How can we know for sure? But the Scripture you just read says there was no room in the inn. Maybe they arrived too late to get a room—or maybe God wanted to highlight their commonness rather than their kingly heritage. Say, I just read about a missionary kid who had a different perspective on the question. Let me see if I can find it. Oh, yes, here it is, from *Our Daily Bread:*

> As a young girl in the late 1920s, Grace Ditmanson Adams often traveled with her missionary parents through inland China. Later, she wrote about those trips and the crowded places where they stayed overnight—village inns full of people coughing, sneezing, and smoking, while babies cried and children complained. Her family put their bedrolls on board-covered trestles in a large room with everyone else.
>
> One snowy night, they arrived at an inn to find it packed full. The innkeeper expressed his regret, then paused and said, "Follow me." He led them to a side room used to store straw and farm equipment. There they slept in a quiet place of their own.
>
> After that, whenever Grace read that Mary "brought forth her firstborn Son, and wrapped Him in swaddling cloths, and laid Him in a manger, because there was no room for them in the inn" (Luke 2:7), she saw the event differently. While some

described the innkeeper as an example of uncaring, sinful mankind who rejected the Savior, Grace said, "I truly believe that Almighty God used the innkeeper as the arranger for a healthier place than the crowded inn—a place of privacy.

What do you think about that, Deena?"

"I think that Grace was right; the cattle shed may have been a blessing in disguise. What a good thing it was for Mary, Joseph, and Jesus to be alone and in a place where the shepherds could find them!"

Chapter 5

Japan and America—1994–2002

Every four or five years, Bible translation missionaries must return to their homeland to reconnect with their sending constituency. Supporters love to hear reports of all that is happening in the missionaries' projects and programs. Often, missionaries need to expand their support base, and the best way to do that is to have face-to-face contact with the people and their supporting churches.

When Deena was four years old, Aylea took Deena for the first time to her own family home in Nagoya, Japan. When Deena was eight, Aylea, Deena, and Carol returned to Japan and then traveled together to the United States. Carol had grown up in northern Indiana, near Shiloh, with devoted Christian parents. Shiloh was the home of Indiana Mennonite University (then Shiloh Mennonite College), and many from the Anabaptist background homesteaded there in the late 1800s. Carol's family was a blessing to the members and enjoyed the fellowship and worship in a rural independent Baptist church, called Sugar Ridge Church because of the sugar maple trees in the area.

Deena enjoyed "Aunt Carol's" family. All missionary kids called their parents' missionary colleagues Aunt and Uncle. Aunt Carol's parents still lived on the farm with many animals. Her brother and his wife had two daughters about Deena's age who embraced her like a real cousin. Later their parents quoted them as saying, "Deena is so cute with her natural dark complexion and curly black hair. Her pearly white teeth really stand out, and she makes everybody smile." Deena felt accepted and loved at home, in the church, and in the community. Although at eight years old Deena did not yet keep a journal, she communicated fervently that she wanted to return to Shiloh next furlough.

At twelve, Deena had an impressive background of knowing and loving people in Papua, Japan, and the United States, and had studied World War II in the sixth grade. When Deena returned to Japan, she contemplated the war Japan had waged against her neighbors and the warm and loving people of Indiana and other states.

"Mommy, why did Japan bomb the United States at Pearl Harbor?"

"That is not an easy question, Deena, but let me share with you an answer from my perspective, and if that does not satisfy, you can do some more library research on your own," Aylea replied. "Before the war, the Japanese Emperor, Hirohito, considered himself a god and demanded reverence and worship. As a god, he felt he had the power to invade other countries and then take over the world. He led Japan when it invaded Korea and China; both were powerless to resist. With war raging in Europe and America poised to enter the war in Europe, Hirohito thought that it was the right time to attack the United States.

"From my perspective, God had a hand in it. Japan was very unwelcoming to missionaries from the United States and Europe, even antagonistic to Christianity. But after the war, the people of Japan realized the Emperor was not a god, and they were more open to hearing the gospel. The story of the founder of our church here in Nagoya, Pastor Jacob DeShazer, is an example of what I am trying to say."

From the book, *DeShazer,* by C. H. Watson

Jacob DeShazer was born in Salem, Oregon, of Christian parents. He attended church with his family, but after graduation from Madras High School in 1932, he went away on his own and did not serve the Lord or have much interest in the church. In fact, in the next six years he worked on farms and ranches all over the west and started his own turkey business, which folded after just one year.

In 1939 Jake joined the Army and trained as an airplane mechanic and bombardier. When Jake heard about the bombing of Pearl Harbor, he became enraged. "The Japs are going to have to pay for this!" he shouted. One day soon after, Jake's superior officer called him to his office. Jake assumed he had done something wrong and would be reprimanded, but when he arrived, there were fifteen or twenty other soldiers already standing around the office. The captain asked them all if they would be willing to volunteer for a very dangerous and secret mission. Every man present agreed and felt honored to have been chosen to be part of "Doolittle's Raiders," named after General Jimmy Doolittle, commander of the group.

For a month, the men were given special training in low-level flying in the dark. Of the sixteen B-25s loaded on the aircraft carrier *USS Hornet*, Jake's was the last to load and was piloted by Lt. William Farrow. Eleven ships in the task force sailed from

San Francisco to a point nine hundred miles east of Japan. The original plan was to sail to a point about four hundred miles out, but at nine hundred miles the Americans met some Japanese ships and decided not to risk the mission with a prolonged battle at that point. On April 18, 1942, the sixteen planes took off, but being farther away from Japan than planned, there was no way they could complete the mission and return to the convoy. It was a one-way trip. The raid was a success, but two planes had to be ditched in enemy territory, including Lt. Farrow's.

After bombing Nagoya, Japan, the number sixteen plane attempted to reach the planned safe airstrip in Choo Chow Lishui, China, but Jake DeShazer and the rest of the B-25 crew were forced to parachute from an altitude of 500 feet into enemy territory over Ningpo, China, when their B-25 ran out of fuel. Jake broke some ribs in the fall, and along with the rest of his crew, was captured the next day by the Japanese. He was sent to Tokyo with the survivors of another Doolittle crew and held in a series of POW prisons both in Japan and China for forty months—thirty-four of them in solitary confinement. Three of the crew were executed by a firing squad, and another died of slow starvation. Jake was severely beaten and malnourished, but God apparently had other plans for him.

During his captivity, Jake persuaded one of the guards to loan him a copy of the Bible. Although Jake only had possession of the Bible for three weeks, the Holy Spirit convinced him that his return to the Lord was God's reason for his survival, and he committed his life to Christ. His conversion inspired him to learn a few words of Japanese and to treat his captors with respect, which resulted in the guards reacting in a similar fashion. Sergeant DeShazer's death sentence was commuted to life imprisonment by Emperor

Hirohito. But on August 20, 1945, DeShazer and the others in the prison at Beijing, China, were finally released when American soldiers parachuted into the compound. Upon his return to the United States after the war, he was promoted to Staff Sergeant DeShazer and awarded both the Distinguished Flying Cross and the Purple Heart for his part in the Doolittle Raid.

Jake enrolled in Seattle Pacific College where his sister was a student and also secretary to the president of the college, and began his studies to be a missionary. He completed his bachelor's degree in three years, and returned to Japan with his wife, Florence, in 1948.

Japan—Summer, 2002

"Deena, do you remember meeting my uncle, Mitsuo Fuchida?"

"Yes, isn't he the airplane pilot?"

"He was. In fact he commanded the bombing raid on Pearl Harbor. Do you know how he became convinced he needed the Lord?"

"No, how?"

"After the war, he was disillusioned and bitter. Then one day in downtown Tokyo someone handed him a leaflet, a tract entitled *I Was a Prisoner of Japan,* the testimony of Pastor DeShazer, and my uncle began reading the Bible for himself. When he came to the words of Jesus on the cross, 'Father, forgive them, for they do not know what they do,' he realized that a powerful transformation had occurred in the life of DeShazer, and my uncle also gave his life to Christ. He spent the rest of his life as a missionary in Asia and the United States. On occasion, Pastor DeShazer and Uncle

Mitsuo preached together as Christian missionaries in Japan. He also led my parents to the Lord and encouraged Pastor DeShazer to return to Nagoya to plant a church there. After six successful years as a traveling evangelist, the Lord led Pastor DeShazer to complete his Master of Divinity degree at Asbury Seminary. When he returned to Japan, Pastor DeShazer decided to reduce his traveling ministry, settle down, and begin to plant churches.

"In 1959, Pastor DeShazer moved to Nagoya to establish a Christian church in the city he had bombed. As you know, that's where my family lived. So we began attending the Free Methodist church he pastored." Aylea paused. "Do you know why I went to Seattle Pacific College?"

"I would imagine it is because Pastor DeShazer went there?"

"Yes. May I tell you one more story where I see God's hand in what happened because of the war?"

"Of course, Mommy, please do!"

"When I was a student at SPC, I took some courses in linguistics, but I wanted to study the Transformational Theory and was told I would have to go to the University of North Dakota for that. So in 1973, I went to UND for the summer session in lingustics. Aunt Carol was my roommate. We found that we really connected with each other and that we would like to be assigned to work on a language together as well. So when we graduated and came to Papua in 1975, we studied the national language together and then were assigned to our language group there. When we first arrived in Papua one of the local officials wanted to show us around a bit and took us up on a mountain that overlooked a large valley. He said, 'Down in this valley was fought one of the bloodiest battles of the entire world war between the Americans and the Japanese.' When he looked again at us, he became embarrassed and turned beet-red—Carol, an American, and I, from Japan.

"What do you think, Deena? I feel like I probably would not be a missionary in Papua—or your mother—if Japan had not bombed Pearl Harbor. How could that have happened without the love and leading of the Lord Jesus?"

Chapter 6

Hillside Central Academy—2004–2008

When Deena turned fourteen, Aylea realized it would be good for her to enroll in the Christian school in the mission headquarters town of Sentani. Boys in her home village began to look for wives when girls were about that age, and Aylea felt Deena was too young to consider marriage. But more than that, Deena was asking for more social interaction with young people of her own age, specifically other missionary children. For her part, Aylea was feeling that the demands of village work—studying the language and translating the Scriptures—were making her home school teaching at the high school level more arduous than she had anticipated.

"Mom, why can't I go out to Sentani and study at HCA?" Deena asked one day that spring.

"Well," Aylea considered, "you are five feet five inches tall and taller than most of the girls here—and even taller than some boys. If I measured to the top of your fuzzy hair, you would be taller than I am. When you finish your assignments for eighth grade next month, we will go to HCA and talk to them about it."

Deena liked the description in the school catalog: "Situated in the foothills shadowed by 8,000-foot-high Mount Cyclops, Hillside Central Academy (HCA) derives its name from its location. (Some people think that the C in HCA stands for 'Christian' since the purpose and reason for existence is to share the gospel.) The park-like campus covers a promontory overlooking central Sentani, just below, and beyond is the main runway of the provincial capital's airport on the shores of beautiful Lake Sentani. Winding up the hillside, a concrete entrance road, not much wider than a broad sidewalk, leads to the campus. Maintenance-free, durable concrete adds to the beauty of the entrance as well as sets the site apart from other development in the area."

Early in Deena's first year at HCA she was given an English class writing assignment to describe the campus. She enjoyed the assignment so much that she started a journal and entered the assignment in the journal.

> October 1, 2004. The first sight you see walking up the promontory hill to HCA is a cemetery to the right. It is a local resident cemetery, but some of the expatriate families have buried their loved ones there. Looking over the wall of the cemetery, the first thing you might see is all the little houses. The richer local people will build a roof and maybe caged walls around the graves of those related to them. After discussing this with a few people, I discovered that they do this to keep the spirit of the dead person inside, otherwise the spirit may curse them or haunt them. Other possible reasons are for decoration or to show how rich the family is. Many of the simpler graves have fresh flowers or melted wax (from burned-down candles) placed there by their loved ones.
>
> Further up the hill is an open field. In the morning

it is usually empty. Sometime in the afternoon, however, boys ranging in age from five to twenty show up to play a bit of pick-up soccer. (Sometimes I ask to play with them when there are other girls who also want to play.) By the time a sunset spreads over the horizon the boys have drifted away. From then until long into the evening, the road becomes nicknamed "Lovers' Lane" or "Hang-out Hill." Many courting couples appear on the hill, and groups of young men will gather with some form of alcohol. I wouldn't normally walk on this road at this time of night because the drunken men may yell at you and even advance toward you. This is not one of my favorite things, so I try to be home before sunset.

Near the top of the promontory, a large gate and small guard house provide security for students, staff, parents, and visitors. The guards will quickly let you in and you keep walking up the school road. The guard shack there is very simple, and you will often find the guards playing a board game or one of them might be sleeping. I have mixed feelings about the gate and guards. On one hand, I would like to be protected from crazy drunks, or even people who wander in and want to get their picture taken with a foreign student. On the other hand, I would like the school to be more open for local friends. Yet we seem so tightly closed. We might be a "light up on a hill," but we aren't a very welcoming light. However, we do have times when many of the locals are invited in for some activity. Also, we have been reminded a few times of the need for safety, because thieves sometimes get in. And the truth is that gates and guard shelters are actually quite common here.

As you walk along the road you pass neatly trimmed bushes and another open field to your left. That field borders on a few rows of short pine trees. Under those trees is one of my favorite places to sit and watch the sunset. After that you pass some teacher housing. There are three buildings with three apartments in each. From there, on either side of the road, the fence and the edge of the hill are about twenty feet away. You then pass the Director's house. After this, you see a large water tower which looks like a medieval castle tower to your left. Right on the other side of the tower is a *pondok*, which is a wall-less little house with a straw (palm frond) roof. It contains two stone tables and a swinging chair. This is also one of my favorite places to sit and watch the sunset.

Across the street is where I live in the brand new hostel for students. Next to that is the old hostel. After passing the hostel, looking to your left, you will see a large open building and beyond that a full-sized soccer field. The open building has two tennis courts in it, but it is also used for *futsal* and basketball games, as well as varying activities for small children. Across from this is the playground. Next to the playground is the lunch room or cafeteria of sorts. This is where the elementary and middle school kids eat. Walking across the parking lot or on a path from the lunch room, you come to the elementary classroom building, which is right across the street from the gym.

Going up some steps, you reach the middle school. Between the middle school and the high school are the library and the multipurpose building. The multipurpose building, housing the nurses' and dental offices, music practice room, and an auditorium used for all-school activities and as a chapel, is prominent. Finally, the high school buildings including classrooms, science and computer labs, and academic offices, all surrounded by flowering shrubs and shade trees, complete the campus.

————————————

Two years later, Deena entered this note in her journal:

April 1, 2006. The high school is already a place of many memories for me. There is a center courtyard with classrooms spaced around it. There are two *pondoks* (palm-frond roofed shelters with picnic tables) located inside. Looking through some classrooms, you can see the fence ending school property and the hill. I can remember sitting at different places for lunches, running from one classroom to the next, laughing on the steps with a group of friends, and cleaning my locker at the end of every year. Also, since it is a place for some social events, I can picture awkward moments, gorgeous sunsets, and pretty dresses. Many afternoons I spent sitting somewhere up there thinking about life or just doing homework. Also, several good conversations have occurred passing in the halls somewhere. Memories are beautiful things to keep.

Excited HCA students who lived in the hostel would tell their parents: "Everyone lives for Friday evening, which is community night." The student athletic teams played teams from other local schools, and one of the senior high classes sponsored the treats for sale, such as tacos, hot dogs, and pizza. Friday night was a great time for the community to get together and enjoy the school activities and catch up with all their friends from town.

———————

Living on campus, Deena was never separated from school. Thus, most of the people and incidents that influenced her and shaped her high school years were somehow related to the school. The HCA teachers made a strong impression on Deena.

April 21, 2007. Though we have many wonderful teachers at HCA, one of my favorite teachers would be Mr. Tom Winslow (himself an MK, missionary kid), my Bible teacher. He has a love for soccer and surfing, which he often talks about. However, due to a bad knee, he can't play soccer anymore. But he still goes surfing a lot, and that is where he says he does much thinking and praying. He is short and balding so is often teased by his students. But he will quickly tease back. It took me a while to realize how much he cares for his students. He wants us to expand our minds, so he challenges us. He wants us to grow, so he tells us the not-so-nice things about us. He wants us to be confident, so he shows us what we could do. Lastly, he wants us to interact with the Papuans, because he has a heart for them also.

Mr. Winslow taught more than how to live the Christlike life. He taught the Word of God. One day while discussing the evolution of theological thought, a student asked, "Does God ever change?"

"Not according to the Scriptures," Mr. Winslow responded. "For example, Malachi 3:6 says: 'For I am the Lord, I do not change; therefore you are not consumed, O sons of Jacob.' And in Hebrews 13:8 we find: 'Jesus Christ is the same yesterday, today, and forever.'"

"Apparently, God does not change, but does He ever change His mind?" Deena asked.

"Good question, Deena. The first instance that comes to mind as I try to answer that question is when Abraham prayed for Lot and his family living in Sodom and Gomorrah, when God revealed to Abraham that He was going to destroy those cities because of their unrighteousness. When Abraham prayed, God promised He would not destroy the cities for fifty righteous people, then for forty-five, then for forty, then for thirty, then for twenty, then for ten. When even ten righteous people could not be found, God found a way to save Lot and his family."

This made Deena think, and she wrote in her journal:

October 5, 2007. Today Mr. Winslow was at his best. Discussing the evolution of theological thought, we went on to talk about 'Does God change' and Scriptural absolutes. Then I asked if God ever changed His mind. The Bible provides several examples of God declaring He would do something, and then someone prayed and God changed His mind. We talked about Abraham and the destruction of Sodom and Gomorrah, Genesis

18:22-33. Then in Numbers 14:10-20 when God told Moses He would destroy the children of Israel. When Moses prayed, God repented and pardoned the people. We also talked about the time when Korah led a revolt (Numbers 16:1-50), when God told Moses to get away from the people so that He could destroy them, and again Moses prayed, and God changed his mind even though many did die. Then we went to James 5:16: 'The effective, fervent prayer of a righteous man avails much.' It makes me wonder, did John the Baptist's disciples pray for him?

Another one of Deena's favorite teachers was Miss Teresa Martino from Spain who taught Spanish, world history, and world geography. Deena described Miss Martino to her mom: "Teresa is tall and dark, with long dark hair and large dark eyes and represents her name and her home area of Cordoba beautifully." After accepting Christ as her Savior in college, Miss Martino wanted to serve as a missionary and heard of opportunities to teach in missionary kids' schools. She joined an international aviation mission agency, and was assigned to HCA for the two years that Deena was a junior and senior there.

Her Castilian accent appealed to Deena who enjoyed distinguishing the various English accents prevalent at HCA— Australian, British, Japanese, Korean, and several American accents. Deena was particularly intrigued with Spanish history aptly detailed by Miss Martino, who highlighted European history that coincided with biblical events.

March 15, 2008. Today Miss Martino made some very interesting comments in her lecture. "The Roman

Empire and its colonizing efforts advanced the spread of Christianity and the growth of the church even as it endeavored to crush the movement through vigorous persecution. In Spain, Roman colonies in Pintia, Clunia, Pollentia, Majorca, and elsewhere encouraged Jews and Christians to come and share their faith. You remember that the Apostle Paul wrote in Romans 15 that he would visit the church in Rome on his way to Spain. These plans were waylaid in Jerusalem, and many historians think that Paul died in Rome. Some, however, feel that Paul did get to Spain and died there." I asked her if she thought that Paul really went to Spain, and she said, "So far, no real evidence that he did has been found, but there are still many places to examine, and someday, someone may yet find the necessary evidence that he did."

One of Deena's most enjoyable and relaxing activities was singing with the student-led worship team. Her beautiful soprano voice combined melodiously with the other leaders, and they appreciated her participation. Many of the songs sung by the group were inspirational and meaningful for her. Her favorite was the song entitled "I've Got a River of Life." The words rang through her mind constantly.

> I've got a river of life flowing out of me,
> Makes the lame to walk and the blind to see;
> Opens prison doors, sets the captives free,
> I've got a river of life flowing out of me.
> Spring up, O well, within my soul!

> Spring up, O well, and make me whole
> Spring up, O well, and give to me
> That life abundantly.

Deena did not understand why she liked it so much—maybe it was because she was alive, while her birth mother had died before she knew about the saving grace of God provided through the Lord Jesus. Or maybe the words reminded her of what the Messiah would do to fulfill the prophecy Jesus quoted during His ministry. Or maybe it was that it reminded her of the Baliem River where she was born because it was a river of life to so many who lived along its banks.

She did not write much about worship team relationships in her journal, but she did write a little about certain group members who fascinated her.

> March 21, 2008. James Park always looks and sounds so spiritual when he stands up front singing. So I was surprised when I read a devotional he wrote in which he said he sometimes feels pride in his singing. He discussed how he felt so good and so Christian, and then he realized his heart was in the wrong place. When I read this, I realized James might not be this perfect guy, but he notices his mistakes and learns from them. Now I've noticed that even when it's not planned he'll throw his thoughts into a song. He'll tell the kids between songs to make the next song their prayer, or to listen to the words of the chorus again. He also often sits in the back, behind other worship team members, sitting or standing with his eyes closed. But it doesn't really matter what

position he is in, or where he is located; you can tell he is completely worshipping God, not for anyone else, but for God. It's pretty cool to watch.

Oh, my heart! Why do you throb so hard when I write or even think about James? Is it because we are both adopted? Is it because we don't resemble our adoptive parents? Or is it because what really matters is being like Jesus?

Deena had a hard time not thinking about James and pondered the phenomenon. James was also adopted. When his parents, both Korean nationals, were in the United States for post-graduate studies in linguistics, they were informed by the mission doctors that they would probably never have children. As they considered their options, a newborn boy of mixed-racial background became available for adoption. The Parks, with the blessing of their home church and the Korean Embassy, jumped at the chance and began the adoption process. By the time James was fourteen and a junior at HCA, he was six feet tall and taller than both his parents.

Deena also considered James's other physical features. With his skin color about the same as hers and tight curly hair from his African ancestors, she felt somewhat akin to him, although neither felt unique or out-of-place in school or church. His Oriental upbringing made her feel comfortable; even so, she was not uncomfortable with any of the diversity that surrounded her. Deena also appreciated James's athletic talents, as he excelled in both basketball and soccer. But it was his love for the Lord and his music ability that were most appealing to her. She captured the lighter side of James by writing a limerick about him.

> There was a young fellow named James,
> Completely surrounded by dames,
> He helped in distress,
> Complimented their dress,
> But couldn't remember their names.

She wasn't discouraged when he did not pay much attention to her. As she told her mom, "Even when I showed the limerick to him, he still did not even give me the time of day."

———————————

One of Deena's other favorite activities was playing soccer. As soon as she entered the school the coach of the girls' team asked Deena if she would play on the team, and she enthusiastically agreed. She enjoyed playing forward attack position and excelled on the field, scoring nearly half of the team's total score throughout both semesters of her junior year. In her journal she wrote about her feelings on the team.

> At a slightly different level, sports are fought here. We are very competitive and will pack the stands for a tournament game. Even so, there are still some students who shine Christ's light on the court or field.

It was the championship game of the final spring soccer tournament of Deena's senior year. The HCA girls had won every game by more than two goals. Deena, playing center forward, had more opportunities to score than her teammates, and she had made the most of each one. STK (*Sekola Tinggi Katolik*), on the other hand, had also dominated in their classification. All fans from both teams realized that both teams were very deserving of the honor of playing in the championship game.

STK girls were unusually tall for Papuan girls, and they appropriated the rough and tumble type of soccer often played at the high school level. HCA, on the other hand, was well-coordinated and played the more "finesse" type of soccer that Coach Jose Ferreira, from Brazil, expected. The HCA girls could handle the "rough and tough" but preferred to anticipate where the ball was going and intercept it instead of body checking the player with the ball.

The city had consented to let the girls play in the professional stadium for the championship game. It was very exciting for both teams to be allowed to play on a well-kept field and in front of fans numbering in the thousands. Fans came for the girls' game and stayed for the boys' final, as well. (The HCA boys, however, had lost in the quarter-final game.)

Although HCA's team included four girls born in Papua, only one, Deena, was of Papuan parents. The local fans were excited about the possibility of the all-Papuan STK team winning the championship from the international-looking HCA team.

The first half started slowly, with both teams feeling each other out, but with just two minutes remaining in the half, STK scored as the left wing crossed the ball to the center, who headed it into the corner of the goal. The second half began with a little more urgency, and HCA began their fast-paced driving and passing. With just over a minute gone, Deena, with the ball at midfield, passed to a midfielder coming up fast on her right. She then faked to the right and went left around the defender and received the return pass just in front of the defending STK back, who could not turn around fast enough, and Deena shot past her and from within the large area kicked it hard past the goalie to her right.

The score remained 1-1 until late in the game, when Deena set up play similar to the one they scored with earlier. This time, however, when the defenders came to her, the midfielder dribbled right through unchallenged for the goal to the left of the goalie. Final score: STK 1, HCA 2.

April 21, 2008. We just won the Capital Area Soccer Championship over the best team in the province. I should feel elated and joyful—and I do—but I also feel sorry for the other girls who did not win, not only the girls from STK, but all those girls who lost in the preliminaries. It could be worse, however. After the game we lined up at center circle for the traditional high fives between opposing players, but our girls immediately began to hug the other team members, thanking them, complimenting their sportsmanship, and extolling their athletic competence. Then, since STK is a Catholic school, our team captain, Holly Henson, an Aussie MK, asked if she could pray for them. She thanked God for STK and asked that He continue to bless them. It seemed like a long time in prayer at midfield, but at the end the fans all jumped up shouting and clapping. It was good that we could play hard and still bless one another. What would it be like if we did not know the Lord?

After the game James came up and congratulated me with a tender hug—very sweetly. I still can't believe it! At least he noticed me on the soccer field. Why not on the worship team?

Just prior to graduation, in a similar contemplative mood, Deena wrote this entry in her journal about her life at HCA:

May 5, 2008. HCA is a school searching for something more. Almost every student would either like to change something or leave for good. This is mostly because of the way Christian living and teaching surrounds us everywhere. Some would say it is crammed into us. Therefore, students tend to head the other direction, ignoring God or just focusing more on other things. Other students, however, question authority, God, and their family's belief.

Teachers at HCA are mainly devoted to the students' success at the academic level. But, being human, they tend to pick favorites or just judge a specific student more. Yet, however each student is regarded, it is an experience we all learn from.

HCA is a fishbowl, a lifetime experience, and a place I feel safe.

Chapter 7

HCA—Spring, 2008

"Mom, my friend Hannah's grandfather wrote a book and it ends with the most heart-wrenching story—let me read it to you:

> One of the other missionary conference team members was Helen. She and her partner, Rose, were translators for the Kayavani speakers in the Amazon area of Brazil. She told a story I have often shared since that time. When she was translating the gospel of Mark, she employed a young Kayavani mother as her translation helper. During the translation effort, this young mother accepted the Lord as her Savior.
>
> After the gospel of Mark was published in Kayavani, the young mother held it up and asked Helen, 'Your mother did not have this book, did she?'
>
> Helen is from Germany and admitted, 'Yes, my mother had this book.'
>
> 'Your grandmother did not have this book, did she?'
>
> 'Yes,' Helen confessed, 'my grandmother had this book.

Then the young mother shared what was on her heart. 'When I was a little girl my grandmother told me that someone was going to come and tell us how to be free from sin and fear. Why didn't someone come and tell my grandmother?'

I personally believe that God did call some young man to go to the Kayavani people and share with this grandmother whom He had prepared to receive the Gospel, but that guy said 'No.' Then two generations later, God sent Helen and Rose to the Kayavani speakers to share the Good News with the granddaughter. From this experience, God again confirmed to me that when He speaks, it is vitally important to listen and obey!

Deena paused after reading. "Mom, why did God allow this guy to cop out on the mission God had called him to?"

"We don't know yet, Deena, but maybe he chose to 'cop out' and was like a modern-day Jonah."

Shiloh, Indiana—Spring, 1941

"Jack, this is the moment you've been waiting for all your life—down one point, ten seconds left, undefeated all year, and in the State Championship game. Here's what we'll do: Since I called time, Jack, you take it out at mid-court and wait until the big guys get set up under the basket, then pass in to Tony. If you have single coverage, Tony will pass it back to you—go to the top of the key, and take your shot at the buzzer.

"If Tony is free, he can bring it down until someone jumps on him, then if Jack is still double-teamed, one of the big guys will be open under the basket for the layup. My feeling is that they have to guard all of us, so Jack will be ready. Okay, Saints—go for it!"

It happened as Coach Olson described—Jack to Tony—back to Jack—a few fakes and Jack was at the top of the key with his unwavering jump shot—swish—and the late foul. With the Saints up one and Jack at the line, the final score was Carrington Colts 82, Shiloh Saints 84.

After the break, Jack and the other starters were called to receive the State Championship trophy. Jack was also named the tournament MVP.

During the next few weeks, Jack was on cloud nine with scholarship offers from Purdue, Indiana University, and Notre Dame. These offers were not only to play basketball, but also football, should he choose, because he had been named 1940 "Mr. Indiana Football" because of all the records he had set as quarterback for the Saints.

He felt like a celebrity but was quickly reminded of his humble background upon returning home. His widowed mother reminded him that she could not help him financially and that he had responsibility to help her and his two younger siblings.

"Jonas David Armstrong," she would proudly say, "I hope all your awards will help you find a job."

Coach Olson knew of Jack's situation at home and looked for a way to help during the summer. His farmer friend from the Mennonite Church, Amos Steinbeck, sometimes needed a farmhand from May to September. Coach explained Jack's situation one Sunday after church.

"Brother Amos, you've heard about my star basketball player, Jack Armstrong, haven't you?"

"Yes, hasn't everyone? Almost too much, but I guess he's deserving."

"Did you know that he comes from a poor family on the south side, that his mother is a widow with three kids to support and can only take in clothes washing and house cleaning when she has the opportunity? Well, he is a strong, intelligent young man who needs a chance to help his mother. Do you have a place for him to work?"

"It's true, sometimes I'm overwhelmed, especially at planting, cultivating, and harvest times. I need help with the early morning and late evening chores. Our farm is a long way from town, but if he could stay in our bunk house and be there with us, I could send his mother twenty dollars each week."

So as soon as finals were over and Jack had graduated, he moved to the Steinbeck farm and began to learn how to help with farming chores. It was long, hard work—from four in the morning to nine or ten at night. Feeding and watering the cattle, horses, pigs, chickens, and goats became tedious, but it was good to be with the animals and in the fresh air. He could feel himself getting stronger every day. But the best part of the job came to be the Steinbeck's eldest daughter, Rachel. Jack could hardly wait for her to come and announce breakfast, dinner, and supper. Rachel, sixteen, was home-schooled and had not heard much about Jack, and Jack had never met or even noticed Rachel before, since she did not frequent school or the Armstrong family's Baptist Church.

But Jack did notice her on the farm. She was beautiful and intelligent, always asking engaging questions about the animals, farm work, and Jack's interests. After he had been on the job about a month, Rachel ventured a question.

"Daddy says you play basketball. Did you ever make a basket?"

"Yes, I made a few, but playing basketball is more than just making baskets. You must get the ball down court to your end and by passing and dribbling—that is bouncing the ball—get it to the place where you or a teammate has a clear shot at the basket. Also you must play defense—that is, keep the other team from scoring."

"How do you do that?"

"You try to intercept a pass, steal the ball when someone from the other team is dribbling, block a shot, or keep the other team from shooting at the basket."

"You seem to know a lot about it. I've got to go now—supper is ready."

"Thanks, I'll be in as soon as I clean up."

Later, during supper, Rachel attempted a comment: "Daddy, Jack says he plays basketball, and he certainly seems to know a lot about it."

"Yes, Coach Olson says that he is the best high school basketball player in the state of Indiana. Have you decided where you are going to college, Jack?"

"Well, I'm thinking about accepting the scholarship offer from Purdue, but Notre Dame is a little closer."

"Yes, but Notre Dame is Catholic. Have you considered Shiloh Mennonite or Taylor?"

"Only a little, because they have not offered any scholarships."

"You may want to think about a Christian school, anyway, where you can get some Bible training, which is most helpful in life." Then, turning to his daughter, he cautioned her: "Rachel, don't you be bothering Jack when he's working."

A month later, when Rachel came to call Jack for supper, he asked, "Rachel, I would really like to get to know you better. Is there some time when we can be together besides meal times?"

"If you would come to church with us, there is always fellowship time when we could be somewhere with young people rather than family. This weekend is the annual missions conference, and Daddy says we will be going both Friday and Saturday nights. You could come if you get your chores done in time."

"Good. I'll ask your dad if I can start chores a little earlier those days."

Actually, when Amos heard of Jack's desire to attend the missions conference, he decided to leave the field early and help Jack with the chores.

The missions conference speaker was a young new missionary from the Mennonite Central Committee to Brazil, but he brought with him an older New Tribes missionary, Fred Brown, who worked among the Indian natives of the Amazon region. On Friday, Pastor Brown spoke on several passages from the Old Testament and the New Testament, showing that the heart of God is burning for the lost, especially those who have never heard the gospel. He shared stories of his visits to various indigenous language groups and their fear of evil spirits and other enemies both natural and supernatural. He highlighted the need among the Kayavani people of the Amazon region and the seeming desire of the people for help and hope.

Jack, enjoying the opportunity just to be with Rachel, actually found himself drawn to the needs among the tribal groups without the gospel, especially the Kayavani, and wondered what he could do to help. He anxiously awaited Saturday's program. Rachel also appreciated the missionary's message, but she was especially intrigued by Jack's desire to follow God's leading to serve Him in bringing the gospel to those who had never heard it.

On Saturday night after a potluck supper at church, Fred Brown's message was "God Has a Plan for Your Life." He shared that God would reveal this plan to those who would open their hearts and completely surrender their all to Him. Pastor Fred again highlighted the needs among the Amazon tribal groups and declared that he felt that God was calling some from the audience in this church to respond to this need. At the close of the service, he asked those who would dedicate their lives to His service at home or abroad to stand and then come forward to kneel at the altar as an act of dedication and surrender to God and His will for their lives.

Jack, sitting in the youth section next to Rachel, whispered emotionally, "I'm going forward. Do you want to also?" Rachel was nervous about her father's probable reaction to her going forward to dedicate her life to the Lord's service in another land. And even worse, it might look like she was doing it because Jack was doing it. Hesitantly, she rose from her seat and followed Jack down the aisle, kneeling beside him at the altar.

After they prayed, Jack was sure God had changed him. His heart was breaking for the lost, and his main goal now was to prepare to serve the Lord on the mission field.

Driving home, Amos did not speak. Jack broke the silence by sharing his newfound leading. "Mr. Steinbeck, God did a work in my heart tonight. I am no longer interested in a scholarship to play basketball, but rather the place where I can prepare by studying God's Word to serve Him on the mission field. You mentioned Shiloh Mennonite College and Taylor College. What do you think about Moody Bible Institute or Fort Wayne Bible School?"

"As a Mennonite, I am drawn to Shiloh Mennonite, but now that I think about you, I would recommend Moody Bible Institute. Really, I am sure you should leave this area, and Moody would be a good place to start." Amos wanted to say more but left it at that. Later, at home, he called Rachel in for a little talk.

"I do not like the influence Jack is having on you. You are too young to be involved with him. I am refusing to let you associate with him anymore. In fact, it is now the middle of August, and I think I will send Jack off to Moody as soon as I can."

The next day, after Amos left to work in the fields, Rachel went out to the barn to find Jack. "Jack, Papa won't let me be with you anymore. I sensed last night that he might react like this, but decided to follow the Lord with you. He says I am too young, but I think he is really afraid I will leave home and go with you to the Brazilian jungle."

"Rachel, I'm sorry. I really care for you. You know we cannot run away together—as much as I would like to. There is no way we could keep seeing each other sneaking behind your dad's back. We must obey your father. The only thing I can do is leave now— he is going to send me away anyhow." He kissed her tenderly, and she went back to the house.

Jack was brokenhearted and angry at Amos Steinbeck. His mind was racing, and like the action-oriented athlete he was, Jack wanted to do something immediately. *I was all right until I committed to missions and the Kayavani people. I just can't face Amos. Maybe I'll join the Army. As a Mennonite, he would be hurt by that. Maybe I should leave right now.* Jack decided to pack his things and hitchhike back to town. When he got there, the driver just happened to let him off in front of the Navy Recruiting Office. Jack was aware that the military was recruiting because of the war in Europe and the rumors of threats from Japan.

I need to find work to help Mom. While I am here I might as well see what the recruiter says. Jack walked in. A good-looking, sharply dressed petty officer approached. "May I help you?"

"My name is Jack Armstrong. I'm needing a job to help my mother. Tell me about the Navy."

"We need strong, intelligent young men like yourself to serve on ships and naval bases that we have on both coasts. You would go to two months of recruit training at Great Lakes, Illinois, or San Diego, California. Then you would be assigned to a ship or base. Or you may be asked to take more training if you're really good at something. What are you good at?"

"Well, I've just quit my job as a farmhand. I know how to take care of animals and milk cows."

"We don't need any farm hands. Anything else?"

"I play basketball."

"Oh, I remember you—the MVP of the state champs! I'm sure you will be able to play a little basketball in the Navy—maybe not on board ships, but elsewhere. If you sign up now, I can get you on tonight's train to San Diego."

"I'll go. Where do I sign?"

———————————

After two months of recruit training and one month of Electronic Technician training, Jack found himself assigned to the battleship *USS Arizona*, headed for Hawaii. On the way, Jack looked up the chaplain.

"Come in, Armstrong. What can I do for you? What's your first name?"

"My first name is really Jonas, but everyone calls me Jack, sir. I'd like to tell you a story and ask a question."

"Go ahead."

"Back in August, I worked for a farmer who has a beautiful sixteen-year-old daughter—"

"This isn't one of those 'farmer's daughter' stories, is it?"

"No, sir. This really happened, and I am miserable. She asked me to go to church with her, and during the missions conference I really felt God calling me to serve Him on the mission field. It was very specific—I was to go to an unreached Indian group in Brazil called the Kayavani people. Her father, my boss, was a little overprotective, and when we both responded to the challenge and committed to go, he refused to let us see each other anymore. I was furious and decided to join the Navy, and here I am, but I feel like Jonah who did not want to be a missionary and joined a ship going the other direction. What do you think—is God mad at me?"

"Your name fits the situation, but God is a gracious God, merciful beyond our imagination and willing to go the extra mile. I would tell Him that you're sorry, ask His forgiveness, and tell Him you will serve him on the Brazil mission field as soon as you finish serving Him on this *USS Arizona* mission field."

"Thanks, Chaplain, I'll do that now."

Jonas David Armstrong was working in the radio room at dawn on December 7, 1941, when the *Arizona* took a direct hit from Japanese bombers in Pearl Harbor. Eleven hundred and seventy-seven crew members died in the attack.

Chapter 8

Indiana Mennonite University— Summer, 2008

The Indiana Mennonite University campus is situated along the south shore of the East Branch River. Early-twentieth-century architecture, maintained even in the more recent facilities, is enhanced by elaborate Victorian houses in the neighborhood. Although perhaps not comparing with other northern Indiana universities such as Purdue, Notre Dame, or even Taylor, Indiana Mennonite University brings tradition to the area and beauty that is unique.

When Deena graduated from HCA in May of 2008, she considered Seattle Pacific University, where Aylea had graduated; Toccoa Falls College, where some of her friends (including Hannah and James) were going; and Indiana Mennonite University, all of which offered her scholarships based on academic achievement and need rather than athletic prowess. She chose Indiana Mennonite because she preferred to be close to the family she knew and loved in Shiloh. Close to downtown Shiloh, the campus was the centerpiece of the town. Deena always felt when she visited Shiloh that it could have been the town featured in the classic movie *Hoosiers*.

When she first arrived in Shiloh from Papua, she stayed with Aunt Carol's brother, Uncle Ron Penner; his wife, Judy; and their two girls, Isabel and Rhonda. Since the girls were still in high school, a senior and a junior respectively, Deena enjoyed a built-in youth group that provided scores of activity and entertainment opportunities. The college-age Bible study discussion group welcomed her, and she appreciated the spirited discussions as well as the attention she received from the guys in the group. Very soon after her arrival, she was asked to join one of the Sugar Ridge Church worship teams—made up of young participants—and succeeded in persuading them to sing some of her old favorites, like "I've Got a River of Life".

"Why do you like this song so much?" one of the team members asked her.

"I've thought about that. I think it is because I like comparing Jesus' words in John 7:38 where he talks about the Holy Spirit— "you shall have rivers of life flowing out of your innermost being"— with the Baliem River, where I was born, since it is a river of life to so many people. It's hard for me to grasp the concept of the Holy Spirit as a river of life, but I know the Baliem River provides water for drinking, washing, irrigating, and transporting—bringing life to many. Does that make sense?"

"Yeah, I think I see your point. And the song is beginning to haunt me also."

Izzy and Rhonda's grandparents lived on the river and invited the youth group to come and enjoy the river and a picnic one Saturday afternoon. When Deena saw the canoes, she jumped in one, barefoot, and, standing near the rear, paddled across the river and back. Some of the young guys immediately challenged her to a race across the river and back. She accepted, and the guys, sitting in the front and back of their canoe, took off. Still standing, Deena quickly caught up with and passed their canoe, pivoting on the rear portion while they were doing a paddle turn, and made it back way ahead of them. The rest of the group roared with laughter while the guys just grinned. In an act of bravado two guys tried to stand and paddle, like Deena, but soon lost their balance and fell in the river. It was a warm day, and they pretended to excuse their clumsiness by saying that they wanted to jump in.

"Where did you learn to do that?" they demanded.

"My village in Papua is on a river like this one, but not as big. There we often travel in dugout canoes that are very heavy and very unstable, but even little guys can stand up and paddle alone."

One evening when Deena's worship team was practicing "I've Got a River of Life", Deena posed this question: "That line that says, 'Opens prison doors, sets the captives free,' what do you think that means?"

The leader responded, "I think it means that Jesus is the river of life, and He frees people who come to Him for salvation."

"So you feel it's a spiritual prison that unsaved people are in, and the freedom is spiritual freedom—freedom from sin's control?" Deena questioned further. "What do you think the prophets meant when they wrote about the Messiah setting prisoners free?"

"Just what prophecies are you referring to?"

"I am thinking of the portion Jesus quoted in Luke 4—I think He was quoting Isaiah 61:1, and He quoted the same verse, or maybe it was Isaiah 42:7, when He responded to John the Baptist's question of what the Messiah was going to do when He came. My question is: What did people *at that time* think the prophet was referring to? Real prisons—like the one John was in—or spiritual prisons that all unsaved are in?"

"When you put it that way, it seems that the people understood the prophet to be talking about real prisons, but we now know that release from spiritual bondage is a reality."

Deena pushed further. "In Luke 7:22, Jesus was referring to the real physical healings He had performed on the sick in the crowd, but He left off the part about freeing the captives—the part John wanted to hear. Why didn't Jesus do what John was expecting the Messiah to do? You can tell I'm not satisfied with the answers I'm getting."

"You're right, Deena. Maybe that's something we'll never know."

———————

Fortunately, with the help of the IMU Admissions Department, Deena was offered a part-time position in the Volunteer Recruitment Office. Her roommate, "cousin" Izzy, also had a job in town for the summer so they were able to ride together. Deena enjoyed her work—calling churches and service organizations, asking for an opportunity to advertise for volunteers, then orienting and assigning those who volunteered to vacancies on campus. Sometimes she would call the various IMU departments to offer the services of a volunteer whom she felt might be able to help them.

One morning, a short, gray-haired lady walked into her office. Deena looked up and greeted her. "Good morning. May I help you?"

"My name is Rachel Steinbeck. I used to teach here in the Missions Department—now they call it Intercultural Studies— and sometimes I'm asked to come back and teach a class when the regular teacher can't make it. But I saw your poster at church last Sunday and thought maybe there would be something else I could do when I have time, which is quite often now."

"How do you do, Dr. Steinbeck? I'm Deena Fuchida. Right now the Development Department is looking for volunteers to help them with their monthly mailing. Things like stuffing envelopes and sticking on address labels. How does that sound to you?"

"I think I could help with that. Should I go over right now?"

"Let me call over there and see what they say. Just a minute." Deena dialed the Development Office. "Dr. Steinbeck, they say that this afternoon or tomorrow morning might be better."

"Okay, Deena, I'll do that—tomorrow morning. Actually I'm not a doctor, just have a master's degree, but I taught here for forty years. But tell me, where are you from, and how did you get to IMU?"

"Thank you for asking. I'm from Papua, and my Aunt Carol Penner is from this area, so I have been here a few times before."

"I heard what you said, but I don't understand—I've lived here all my life, and please do not be offended, but I do not know any other Penners who look like you."

"Of course—I'm adopted. My birth mother died way out in the Papuan jungle right after I was born because of a snake bite, and my father asked my mother, Aylea Fuchida, to adopt me because he could not take care of a baby. Aunt Carol is my mother's partner in the Bible translation project." Understanding flooded Rachel's face, so Deena continued, "My major will be Intercultural Studies—I'll be a freshman this fall. May I ask you, Dr. Steinbeck, why did you study missions and then go on to teach missions?"

"When I was sixteen, a missionary came to our church who challenged us to commit to the Lord's service as a missionary, and I responded. Because a certain young man did also, my dear daddy did not like it and refused to let us continue with this plan. So I obeyed my dad and just studied and taught missions. And I feel the Lord multiplied my efforts by sending many from here to the mission field. I appreciate that I had a small part in making that happen. I'm grateful I can still serve. Where do you go to church here, Deena?"

"Aunt Carol's brother, Uncle Ron Penner, and his family go to Sugar Ridge Church, out in the country. I really enjoy it there and sing with one of the worship teams."

"Yes, I know that church very well. I'll come over and hear you sometime. Thanks again, Deena. Bye."

"Bye-bye. Wait—one more question—I've often wondered why God let my mother die and let me live. Have you ever wondered why He did not let you go to the mission field?"

"Yes, I have. Maybe someday we will understand. I have to go now, but tomorrow I'll help at the Development Office."

The part-time position afforded time for Deena to work out with the girls' soccer club and play some scrimmages. She could tell that these girls played at a higher level than the girls in Papuan high schools, but she felt comfortable playing with them. Since she did not come to college to play soccer, she felt no pressure to make the team and freely enjoyed the competition and the exercise.

One afternoon in early August, a girl well-known by the upperclassmen but new to Deena came and practiced with the team. Afterward, Deena went over and introduced herself. "Hi, I'm Deena. Where are you from?"

"I'm Mia Morgan. I'm from here in northern Indiana, but I have just returned from Spain so I haven't been able to come out for practice until now."

"That is so neat! One of my high school teachers was from Spain and created in me a deep desire to go there. What were you doing in Spain?"

"I went on an archeological dig at an old Roman colony."

"Cool! Which dig did you go on, and did you like it?"

"I went to the Roman amphitheater dig in Clunia, in northern Spain. I loved it! It was the experience of a lifetime. The other team members were quite wild—drinking every night—but I loved the opportunity to do live research, finding things left two thousand years ago."

"Tell me. How did you get interested in archaeology?"

"Well, my dad is Professor Morgan, and he teaches Anabaptist History and Distinctives here at IMU. Every summer he leads a small student group to an archaeological dig somewhere in the United States. So I am naturally interested in archaeology. Since I wanted to go someplace Dad had not already talked about at home, he suggested Israel or one of the ancient Roman sites. I thought the one in Spain sounded exciting, so I went there."

"Wow! Maybe I'll sign up for his course."

"Good idea, but as a freshman, you'll need special permission because it is a 300-level course."

"Thanks, Mia. This makes me *so* excited!"

———————————

From Deena's journal:

> August 3, 2008. Hooray!! I met the neatest girl this afternoon on the soccer field. She is Dr. Morgan's daughter and has just returned from a one-month archaeological dig in Spain! She was part of a team digging the site of an old Roman amphitheater! How exciting! I wish I could have gone with her. Wouldn't Miss Martino be surprised? I just looked at the website.

On the website **www.findadig.com/digs/clunia,** Deena found:

> For archaeologists, few things are more exciting than excavating an entire city that belongs to a single period. Without earlier or later epochs to get in the way, such remains become a direct window into the past, a way for archaeologists to see precisely how a specific group of people built, occupied, and then ultimately abandoned a city.
>
> The Roman city of Colonia Clunia Sulpicia in northern Spain presents archaeologists with precisely this dream scenario. Founded as an administrative center after the Roman conquest of northern Iberia in the early first century BC, Clunia was built not on the nearby ruins of the Iron Age Celtiberian stronghold, but instead was founded as an entirely new settlement

atop a dominating plateau 3,400 feet above sea level. From this majestic point overlooking the Spanish countryside, Clunia became a center of Roman life and culture for the next three-and-a-half centuries. Surveys and excavations have revealed all the wealth and grandeur of a major Roman city, including luxurious public baths, magnificent mansions, a large forum, colossal temples, and beautifully laid out mosaic floors and countless documents that tell us about the life and times of the forty thousand people who walked the streets of Clunia.

The site is perhaps most renowned for its impressive Roman theater, which incorporated innovative architectural elements as well as an intricately designed water drainage system. With an estimated seating capacity of over nine thousand, the ancient theater is the largest ever to be discovered in the Iberian Peninsula. This summer, volunteers at Clunia will help piece together exactly how this impressive Roman theater was built and then transformed over the centuries.

Deena was not able to get into Dr. Morgan's class fall semester, but she did coax him to allow her in for spring semester. She was not disappointed in the class. On February 8, 2009, Deena sent in her application for the dig at Clunia. The application required an application fee of three hundred dollars, which she normally would not have had available, but since her heart had been set on this adventure since August, she had been saving the money from her part-time job. What would she do about the remaining twenty-one hundred dollars required for the program? Mia reminded her of a scholarship offered by *Biblical Archaeology Review,* which required the submission of a letter requesting consideration to the magazine's editor, Dr. Hershel Shanks.

IMU—Fall, 2008

Besides enrolling in the usual freshman core courses, Deena was able to get into New Testament Survey, a required course from the Biblical Literature Department. Undaunted, Deena continued her relentless search for what she called "the rest of the story," and throughout the section called Harmony of the Gospels, she posed her customary questions about John the Baptist. But Professor Yoder could not come up with any new or satisfying answers for her.

In their study of Acts of the Apostles, she carefully worded questions that would help her capture the rest of the story. For example, in Acts 5, when Ananias and Sapphira died, she asked, "I know that Peter called it 'lying to the Holy Spirit,' but did they really intend to lie to the Holy Spirit or just to the apostles and the community?"

"Well, Deena, God seemed to take it personally. We understand that God sometimes reacts with anger, and this time no one prayed for mercy on them. Furthermore, He could have decided that the apostles needed a strong deterrent to keep others from falling into, or yielding to, the temptations of the Devil."

The next day, when they reached Acts 12 and the story of the angel freeing Peter from the Jerusalem prison, Deena asked, "Among the details Luke mentions are the name of the owner of the house where they were praying for Peter's release, Mary, and her son, John Mark, as well as a girl named Rhoda, who was familiar enough with the house and its owners to take it upon herself to respond to a knock at the gate. In the very next chapter, John Mark left Paul and Barnabas in Asia Minor and returned home to Jerusalem. Do you think John Mark's return had anything to do with Rhoda?"

"I like when the young ladies ask questions because they have insights the guys would not consider! We know that Paul was quite upset about John Mark's leaving, and maybe Paul had previously experienced similar turmoil over relationships that would justify his feelings about John Mark abandoning the mission. We also know, however, that he later recognized John Mark's value to his ministry. What do you think?"

"I would like to think that travel difficulties or relationship problems with his mentors would not keep John Mark from continuing on the mission. I think he was sick—homesick, physically sick, or lovesick."

When they reached Acts 18:18—that is, when Paul left Corinth, hiked to the coastal town of Cenchrea, shaved his head ('for he had made a vow'), and sailed to Ephesus—someone requested Dr. Yoder to explain vows. From her experience, Deena knew that sometimes classmates asked questions so the teacher would not have enough time to throw a pop quiz at them or just to slow down the lecture, giving students time to catch up. She appreciated the question, however, because it was on her mind too.

"Vows seem to be a Jewish custom, occurring several times in the Old Testament," Dr. Yoder responded. "Vows generally fall into three types. There were vows of devotion—when an individual praying for something special would vow to devote, set apart, or sanctify a possession, such as money, property, cattle, slaves, or even children to the Lord. You remember Hannah devoted Samuel to the Lord. There were also vows of abstinence. The Nazarites vowed abstinence from partaking the fruit of the vine in any form, from cutting their hair or beard, and so on. Samson and John the Baptist were Nazarites. And finally there were vows of destruction. God decreed that certain things were dedicated for destruction. For instance, images of foreign gods were to be utterly destroyed. In the conquest this occurred; as the children of Israel conquered, they were to destroy all or certain objects of plunder.

"In Paul's case, most scholars believe that he had taken a vow of abstinence, and when he arrived in Cenchrea, the vow came to an end and he shaved his head. Others feel that it must have been something else since Paul was the apostle to the Gentiles, and they would not have understood this Jewish tradition. What do you think? Anyone care to venture another possibility? Deena?"

"This is more of a question than a response to your question—but I think the town may be important. It is mentioned at least one other time in the Bible. In Romans 16:1, Paul recommends Phoebe, a resident of Cenchrea, to his friends at the church in Rome. He said that she had tenderly helped him and others. Could it be that she had something to do with the vow? That he somehow abstained from doing something she desired? Why didn't Luke clarify these things?"

"I love your feminine insight. You may have something there. We do not know—it's one of those mysteries. Time to go—class dismissed."

The next day the class reached verses 24–28 of Acts, chapter 18, introducing Apollos in Ephesus who knew only about John's baptism and the Lord Jesus. Picking up on Deena's curiosity, another student, Dan Kroeker, raised a question. "Since Apollos was from Alexandria, in northern Africa, how had he learned about John the Baptizer's baptism and Jesus? Could an apostle have taught there? Early church tradition has it that St. Thomas went to India, and Joseph of Arimathea went to Britain, but it seems like if one had gone to Alexandria, he would have told the converts about the baptism of the Holy Spirit. Am I right?"

"I think you are right, Dan, but the question, 'How did he learn what he knew?' still remains." Then, feeling that Dan was asking Deena's questions for her (after they had discussed the assignment together)—"How do you think it happened, Deena?"

"Apollos was a Jew with a Greek name. I think as a young man he made a pilgrimage to Jerusalem for the Passover, and while he was there heard about John the Baptizer, went out to the wilderness to see him, and was baptized by him there. He could have even been John's disciple for a while. This could have been about the time Jesus was baptized so he also heard about Jesus, the Messiah, but not about the baptism of the Holy Spirit."

"You certainly have a very possible solution, Deena; maybe someday we will know how it all happened." Dr. Yoder continued, "We know that Apollos was a dynamic speaker and gained a large group of followers in the church at Corinth. Paul sensed that the enemy used certain distinctives between Apollos and himself to create division among the church members and pleaded passionately with the church to lift up only the Lord Jesus. The Corinthian conflict did not seem to influence these two powerful men of God to be at odds with each other, for we find in Titus

3:13 that Paul asked Titus to help Apollos and Zenas on their trip, possibly to travel across the Greek peninsula to see Paul in Nicapolis."

Deena was pleased with the answer to one other question in the Book of Acts. Dr. Yoder's lecture included his admiration of Luke's description of Paul's voyage to Rome with the details of the storm and the shipwreck itself.

Dr. Yoder began. "Luke as a physician either knew something of ocean travel or learned much about it during this trip because he uses many nautical terms in the book that you would not have expected an ordinary person to use. His description of the shipwreck is interesting. I'll read it to you beginning from Acts 27:27.

> "Now when the fourteenth night had come, as we were driven up and down in the Adriatic Sea, about midnight the sailors sensed that they were drawing near some land. And they took soundings and found it to be twenty fathoms; and when they had gone a little farther, they took soundings again and found it to be fifteen fathoms. Then, fearing lest we should run aground on the rocks, they dropped four anchors from the stern, and prayed for day to come. And as the sailors were seeking to escape from the ship, when they had let down the skiff into the sea, under pretense of putting out anchors from the prow, Paul said to the centurion and the soldiers, "Unless these men stay in the ship, you cannot be saved." Then the soldiers cut away the ropes of the skiff and let it fall off. And as

day was about to dawn, Paul implored them all to take food, saying, "Today is the fourteenth day you have waited and continued without food, and eaten nothing. "Therefore I urge you to take nourishment, for this is for your survival, since not a hair will fall from the head of any of you." And when he had said these things, he took bread and gave thanks to God in the presence of them all; and when he had broken it he began to eat. Then they were all encouraged, and also took food themselves. And in all we were two hundred and seventy-six persons on the ship. So when they had eaten enough, they lightened the ship and threw out the wheat into the sea.

"When it was day, they did not recognize the land; but they observed a bay with a beach, onto which they planned to run the ship if possible. And they let go the anchors and left them in the sea, meanwhile loosing the rudder ropes; and they hoisted the mainsail to the wind and made for shore. But striking a place where two seas met, they ran the ship aground; and the prow stuck fast and remained immovable, but the stern was being broken up by the violence of the waves. And the soldiers' plan was to kill the prisoners, lest any of them should swim away and escape. But the centurion, wanting to save Paul, kept them from their purpose, and commanded that those who could swim should jump overboard first and get to land, and the rest, some on boards and some on parts of the ship. And so it was that they all escaped safely to land."

"Dr. Yoder," Deena interrupted, "Luke's description says that they left the anchors in the sea at a place different from the rest of the shipwreck. Do you think that they may still be there? Has anyone tried to find them?"

"Interesting you should ask, Deena. I recently read a book on that subject by Dr. Robert Cornuke, entitled *The Lost Shipwreck of Paul,* which tells of his adventures looking for the anchors. The interesting thing is that they had already been found and recovered from the place Luke described, but since the Government of Malta would prosecute anyone owning Maltan historical artifacts or relics, these divers kept them hidden. In the book, Dr. Cornuke tells how the government was persuaded to provide amnesty to those who had the anchors, and now they are in a museum for everyone to see and appreciate."

IMU—Spring, 2009

One day during spring break, Deena, together with Grandma Penner, was invited to tea at Rachel Steinbeck's home. For the occasion, Deena chose her yellow IMU pullover with her favorite Indonesian batik scarf draped around her neck in the current fashion. Another lady, Mary Walsh Carlson, whose parents were former missionaries in Brazil and old friends of Rachel's, was the special guest. As the four sat around the table, Mary explained that she had been adopted as a small girl, and shortly thereafter her parents returned to the United States where her father took a position as a Mennonite pastor. Thus they were known to Rachel and her family.

Mary turned to Deena. "I understand that you also were

adopted by a single missionary lady, Aylea Fuchida. How do you feel about that?"

"Well, I think I understand the stress or even distress that some adoptive kids go through. For example, some are plagued with the question, 'Why did my parents abandon me?' But with me, it was different. I always knew why I was adopted, and grew up in a loving and privileged home. What a gift—to learn four languages at home, and to have access to the finest education with dear friends from all over the world. I do have some nagging questions, mainly spiritual, such as, why did God allow me to survive as an infant and be so blessed? How was it for you?"

"My birth parents were killed in a tragic automobile accident, and my sister, Carla, and I were adopted—Carla by another missionary family from our church in Brazil and I by the Walshes. We both married and have families who love and serve the Lord, but still some nagging thoughts, like yours, remain: Why did God allow this in our lives?"

"Do you know of others who have been adopted and went from rags to riches, so to speak?" Deena asked, interested to hear more.

"I know of several thrilling instances where families have adopted four or five siblings. In one case, a family from Illinois who already had four children of their own heard about a family of five in an orphanage, went to Brazil, and adopted them. A few years later, they heard of another family of five and adopted them also.

"Let me share another dramatic instance. About thirty years ago, a mission pilot flew cargo to a remote Indian village. While he was there, the village leaders decided they could no longer care for two small orphans, an older sister about six and a younger brother about four. So they decided to throw them in the piranha-infested river to let them drown or be eaten by the piranhas. They did that while the pilot 'just happened' to be there. Of course he jumped in the river and rescued the two children. He took them home, named them Lydia and John, and adopted them. He and his wife already had two children of their own about the same ages as the two he rescued."

"Does that happen very often—that is, people leaving children to die?"

"It's not as rare as we might think, especially when the kids are handicapped in some way. Last year I watched a video, produced in Brazil, about a small, club-footed native girl living in a village where they wanted to do away with her because it took a lot of time and energy for someone to take care of her. So they took her way out in the jungle and left her there. She could not walk. Her big brother, about thirteen, also on crutches, went out and found her. He knew he could not bring her back to the village since they wanted to be rid of her, so he carried her for several days through the jungle to the home of a missionary he knew.

"You will be interested in this, Deena, because the missionary's name is Subaru. His father, like Aylea, found the Lord in Japan after the war and immigrated to Brazil to share the gospel with the Japanese immigrants there. The son became a missionary to the natives living in remote jungle villages. God inspired young Subaru to take up the plight of children, especially underprivileged native children who are rejects of the community or handicapped in some way. He founded an organization that is providing shelter and hope for these kids and their parents who love them."

Changing the subject, Rachel asked Deena to tell about her upcoming summer adventure. Deena shared her plans to participate in the archaeological dig at Clunia, Spain, and the possibility of finding evidence of the spread of the gospel in that area. Then she asked the ladies to pray that the Lord would provide the funds needed to pay for the program costs—that is, if she was not granted a scholarship—and the cost of the flight over and back.

"I've been meaning to mention that God has prompted me to help you with the airline tickets, if the scholarship does come through," Rachel promised.

Chapter 9

Roman Archaeological Dig—
Tuesday, June 30, 2009

"How are you feeling this morning, Deena? Are you excited about this adventure in Spain?"

"It's all new for me, Mom. We've had several international adventures together before, but this time I'll be alone—not really alone, of course—but without someone familiar to rely on and have confidence in. On the other hand, Mia Morgan has given me a very ample picture of what to expect, and in some ways I feel like I've already been there. What about you, Mom?"

"Yes, this is different," Aylea agreed. "You know five years ago when I left you at HCA alone and went back to the village? You really weren't alone—with all your 'uncles and aunts,' our missionary colleagues, and most of the kids at school you already knew—although it's different living with them at the hostel. Then last year when I left you at IMU, you had Carol's family whom you know and love, and they love you. Now, this time, you know no one, but it's only for one month, and you could come home early if you really had to. Still, I am a little overwhelmed. I must 'trust and obey' as the old hymn says."

"My flight leaves from Michiana Airport at 3:00, so we'd

better get there about 1:00. It's interesting that the airline gave me less than an hour layover in Chicago, barely enough time to get from the United Express gate to the international terminal."

"Looks like we arrived plenty early!" Aylea exclaimed, glancing at the departure schedule board. "Flight 1442 to O'Hare is a half hour late."

"That leaves me less than a half hour to make my connecting flight to Spain—just another opportunity to trust the Lord for peace and assurance. I hope I have time to find and meet Sharon, the other dig group member from Chicago!"

Wednesday, July 1, 2009

Actually, it was worse than all her fears (from Deena's journal):

July 1, 2009. The trip over was absolutely ridiculous! Mom, you should have seen me running like crazy through the Chicago airport just to reach the gate on time—I was still late. PTL, they waited for me, but then I was unable to connect with Sharon, and I worried about that. It seemed like a long all-night flight to Madrid and I hardly slept—and it's not like I haven't taken long flights before. Must be the excitement of actually participating in the dig program.

We arrived in Madrid this morning about 7:30 a.m. God is good, and I met an American exchange student on the same flight. Thankfully, together we found our way to the luggage claim area, and it was there that Sharon found me. She is a very sweet, soft-spoken

20-year-old—and an anthropology and history major at Loyola University in Chicago. We connected right away—PTL. We waited and waited, but my luggage never came—so after going to get help, I was told it would be coming in the next day, since it was still in Chicago! Thank the Lord I put extra clothes in my carry-on!

Finally we made our way to the meeting point—a bus ride to the other side of the airport. We were early, but so tired. We just sat on a park bench and watched the people go by. I did get some money out and bought a bottle of water. The other group members finally showed up—Jennifer from Australia, archaeology major; Carla from New Mexico, archaeology major; Kayla from New York, biology major; Rick from Ohio State, classics major; and Luke from San Francisco, Stanford University, physics major, classics minor.

Deke Jones and Sophia Cortez (dig leaders) picked us up, and we headed out. They drove us in their own cars (Deke drives a white Landrover—the typical vehicle you would see in the movies for an archaeologist!—and Sophia drives a small VW). I was in the VW with Sophia, Jennifer, and Carla. We stopped at El Recinto Amurallado de Buitrago del Lozoya for lunch. It was a medieval town which is now being restored. In the town is an old castle, but the inside of the castle was reconstructed into a bullfight ring in the mid-twentieth century. The weather here is very hot—like Papua.

Lunch of the day at this Spanish pub was pork, deep-fried seafood, French bread, and water. Between lunch and Clunia, we stopped for groceries at a bigger town, in a store similar to Wal-mart. Sadly, alcohol seems to be the beverage of choice—very important to many people here—wine for almost every meal and beer for a social drink after the meal. I guess it's the European culture. But God is so good—I'm afraid it's quite evident even from the beginning that I am the only team member claiming to be an evangelical Christian, and also the youngest.

The group finally arrived in Clunia. Driving up to the small town, they could see the remains of the theater, five huge brick structures still standing. For Deena, it was hard to imagine what it might have been like back in its day, even more impressive than Mia described. Sonia, acting as a guide, explained, "The amphitheater would have been three times higher than we see it, because the Romans were very extravagant and liked to show their wealth and power. And therefore they erected the theater in this place for a reason, so that those traveling into the town would be amazed and impressed."

Housing for the English-speaking team consisted of a large, three-story house divided into three apartments, or flats. The first floor was occupied by the landlord and his family. Sophia, Jennifer, Carla, and Kayla lived in the second floor flat. Sharon and Deena were assigned a room in the third floor apartment with Deke, Rick, and Luke. After climbing the stairs to the third floor, they entered a hallway with bedrooms, two to the right, Deke's and Rick's, and two to the left, Luke's and the girls'. At the end of the hall to the right was an open area furnished with a small table and four wooden straight-backed chairs. On the other side, two couches, two easy chairs, and a TV filled up the rest of the room.

Beyond this open dining/living area was the tiny kitchen, with a small fridge, sink, gas stove, cupboard, and small table.

At the very end of the hall to the left of the entry was the bathroom, which included a sink, urinal, toilet, washing machine, and tub with a hand-held shower head. Sharon and Deena's room was furnished with two single beds. On each window were outside shades that could be pulled open or closed from the inside. The shades had little slits that still let some light and air in, yet kept most of the bugs out.

I am rooming with Sharon, but sharing the flat with Deke, Rick, and Luke. I'm not sure how all of that worked out and not even sure how I feel about it. Mia did not tell me about this! I have never lived with so many boys of this type. (The five at the hostel were, or at least seemed to be, my brothers. None of these three holds a candle to James.) I am not sure if it's because of me or what, but Sharon and I are the only ones who have yet to drink. Kind of a support system, I guess.

I am completely overwhelmed, exhausted, and a little frustrated. I don't have any clothes or supplies since my luggage is still not here. It's supposed to come tomorrow! Thankfully Sharon is letting me use some of her stuff.

The Bible verse rings true: "The joy of the Lord is my strength." I feel like that is all the strength I have right now. Also plaguing me is the question: Why was this prosperous Roman city abandoned or destroyed?

Thursday, July 2, 2009

The next morning, Deena woke up about 8:00. She had slept well in her old, squeaky bed, and then enjoyed a fast, light breakfast of a muffin and orange juice. About 9:00 a.m. at the equipment shed, the students filled wheelbarrows full of equipment, walked it all to the site, and started digging the first layer of dirt off of the north side of the theater area. The equipment included a shovel, pickaxe, wheelbarrow, trowel, plastic bucket (to put artifacts in), and a whisk-broom/brush. It was hard work. The teams were divided into groups of three: one person with the pickaxe, another with the shovel, and the last with the wheelbarrow. The volunteer worker with the pickaxe would loosen the hard-packed soil for a while until there was enough loose dirt to fill a wheelbarrow, and then the person with the shovel would come in and shovel all the loose dirt into the wheelbarrow. The person with the wheelbarrow would then push it to the dirt pile and dump it. Then the routine would start all over again.

They worked from 9:00 to 11:00, at which time they enjoyed a snack of leftovers from the night before. After break they went back to work until they finished with the first layer which, as described by Deena, was "full of weeds and dirt, or dirt and weeds." Once that was finished, the Spanish Director, Dr. Hernando Torres, wanted a picture of the completed work and then announced they were done for the day.

July 2, 2009. What we found in our work today: column pieces and ceramic pieces (the ceramic pieces with a stamp mark on them or drawing are the pieces they keep). We also found many pieces of roof tile, but because they have found so much of that they no longer keep it. They have discovered four different types and sizes of columns. One set was used in the back of the theater where the viewers sat. Then at the front of the theater, because it had many layers, there were at least two different columns depending on what tier/level they were constructed. Then there were two huge columns on either side of the stage near the center. It is interesting because the archaeologists know exactly what the different sizes and shapes are; the Romans were so precise in their measurements that with just a small piece of a column the archaeologist can determine the actual size.

After the crew packed up the equipment, they went for drinks at the local bar for visitors and workers, just a few feet away from the site. After the hard work, Deena enjoyed her cold glass of Coke immensely. Since it was about 3:00 p.m., the team drove to Huerta, a town about five minutes away, for lunch. At the bar selected, lunch was three courses and the biggest meal of the day. First course: macaroni pasta with seafood; second course: choice of beef, chicken, or fish; and third (dessert) course: ice cream, fruit, cake, or rice pudding.

After our 3:00 p.m. lunch, we took an hour to rest and relax. I feel completely exhausted and overwhelmed, just trying to remember all the info and details. After our siesta, about 4:30, we were off again for a tour of Clunia, the city and theater. It was very impressive.

The whole city was built on a plateau. The first time archaeologists started digging was in the 1930s. So far what has been revealed are the community baths, an elaborate mansion, and the central forum.

The baths consisted of a large building with a large courtyard entrance. There were two identical sides—one for women and one for men. The first room was more of a social meeting or workout room. The second room was the changing room. The third room was the cold bath, and the fourth room was the warm bath. Then the two sides came together to a shared hot bath room.

The mansion excavation was one of the first to be uncovered, but it suffered because in the 1930s they replaced missing artifacts in places they just thought "looked good," not necessarily where they would have been at the time of construction. It has, however, a huge foundation with beautifully detailed flooring murals, still very well preserved.

The forum consisted of a large courtyard with a roof held up by columns. On either side of the courtyard were small shops. Archaeologists have dug up one side, yet have kept the other side under soil to preserve it. (It should be identical to the side already excavated.) On one end was a large temple built to worship the god Jupiter.

The directors explained that when archaeologists first came, the amphitheater was covered with grass and even trees growing all around in it. After the plants and trees were removed work started on the stage area. Previous teams had excavated dirt to about ten feet below where it was originally found, except for the north side where Deena's team started clearing this year. The amphitheater was originally constructed to be a theater for dramatic presentations. Since Romans delighted in extreme measures and built elaborately, the theater was built to impress, and it was the first thing people would see coming into the city. Later the Romans renovated it to make it into an arena. As Mia had already explained to Deena, twenty gravesites behind the theater were found and excavated the previous year.

The Romans chose this area to build Clunia not only because of the high plateau (they could see for miles, see if enemy was coming), but also because of an available natural underground water source.

I loved the tour. I felt like I was back in time as I sat and gazed out over the vast patchwork of farmland, hills, mountains, and trees of yellow, brown, red, and green. It's as if the Lord placed a soft, warm quilt over this whole area. It's beautiful and breathtaking. No wonder the Romans settled here. From this view I can see for miles. I like to take in deep breaths. The air is so rich and fresh; there is almost a special purity to it. It's as if the world of today (technology, pollution) has not yet contaminated it, and this one area remained back in time. I feel like I am the main character in the book *The Mark of the Lion*, walking through the baths and the city. The Romans were so intimidating; it would have been scary, for me, to have been a Christian walking through the city, sharing the love of Christ.

<u>What I learned on the site today:</u>

1. How we are to use the wheelbarrow—Deke: "One rule to remember—don't push with your thighs, because it could cut or bruise them."

2. How we are to use the pickaxe: Bend knees, bend at waist, and only use your arms. Put your dominant hand at the neck of the axe and your non-dominant hand at the base of the handle. Lift and swing the axe up with your arms, then let the axe with its heavy metal top part do all the work on its own. As the axe falls, slide your dominant hand down the handle to meet non-dominant hand at base of handle.

We went to dinner at 9:00 p.m. I went to bed at eleven. Others went out to the bar. I still don't have my luggage. Hopefully tomorrow!

Friday, July 3, 2009

Deena didn't sleep very well because Sharon was up most of the night, her neck bothering her, and, as a result, Deena was up with her. In the morning Sharon asked Deke to take her to the clinic. She was gone all day. After she came back from the clinic, she stayed at the flat and slept. The doctor said her pain was caused by pulled neck muscles.

At the site the routine was the same as the day before but this day they started digging a trench, a three-dimensional rectangle with the same team organization—that is, in groups of three.

The three of us kept working; I mostly shoveled or pushed the wheelbarrow. I think my favorite is the wheelbarrow, like working on the airstrip back in the village. On the way to the dirt pile I am able to have time alone, pray, sing, just enjoy the scenery. Shoveling is hard work. I have not gotten the knack of tossing the dirt with the shovel yet, and my back is so weak it doesn't take long for it to start hurting. Pickaxing is fun, yet tiring. Although today while I was pickaxing, I dug up a huge piece of column. Deke was impressed, especially since I almost tossed out a small piece of column earlier in the day thinking it was only a rock! Oops! But that was the highlight of my day—digging up the huge piece of column!

Deena and her English-speaking team enjoyed working alongside the Spanish-speaking team, one of whom was the Director, Dr. Hernando Torres. Another was archaeologist Sophia Cortez, doing her master's on the underground water source. She explored the wells scattered around the city of Clunia and found a very intriguing shrine in one of the underground wells. Another Spanish Director, Jose Fonseca, appeared as if cast for the role, with long black hair down to his waist, a mustache, and goatee as well as sideburns.

Today, Dr. Hernando Torres, director of the whole project, was here with his fourteen-year-old son. Dr. Torres is a university professor, and he sure looks the part! He is about five-foot-ten, thin, with graying black hair almost down to his shoulders. He has a large prominent nose, glasses with thick, square lenses, and a long thick mustache and bushy eyebrows!

At 1:30 we stopped working for lunch and went to the same bar for another three-course meal. I had the fish, potato salad, and yogurt with fruit. We are all so tired that during most of the meals there is no conversation—we just sit and stare at each other. The Spaniards usually talk—obviously in Spanish—so most of us are not part of their conversation.

I am very tired, yet the Lord is sustaining me. He is so good! I am so thankful I know Him, as it is difficult being in this type of atmosphere. I am used to being in Papua, a somewhat dangerous place, yet there I am surrounded by fellow believers and have amazing support and a common bond. Here, it's a safe place, yet I am surrounded by unbelievers. It's hard to say, but in some ways I almost prefer a dangerous place being with believers than a safe place being with unbelievers; things are so much easier with believers. The Lord has me here for a reason—maybe to give me confidence in Him for some future program—and I feel it's my duty and desire to show His love to these people. They are all very nice, considerate, fun people, yet they are also lost and in need of God's love. Please, Lord, help me to be bold and confident in the Lord's work. "I've got a river of life flowing out from me."

The site work is fairly easy, in terms of mental work, yet it's obviously physically exhausting. I am grateful I am a visual learner, since learning to dig is all visual and practice. I have many blisters on my hands already and I am sure many more to come.

PTL, my luggage came today! I am very thankful.

I feel as though I am becoming a mother hen to Sharon. She is very homesick and not feeling well. I feel for her, yet am also very thankful for her, since we are similar in many ways. We are both quiet, like to work hard, be organized, and seem to keep to ourselves. She seems to stay fairly close. Last night she asked to stay with me instead of going to the bar; it was nice to have her company!

Sharon is also having a hard time because her grandpa is in the hospital. I think she is thinking of going home, but I hope not. She will be missed, and then I will be left all alone with those boys on the top floor and I don't know how I feel about that! (I e-mailed Mom and my friends, Hannah and James. I'm so glad James is actually interested in hearing about this adventure and is praying for me!) So we all are praying for Sharon. Her neck still hurts, and she is just having a hard time.

Saturday, July 4, 2009

By 8:00 a.m. they were back at the amphitheater dig site when Dr. Hernando appeared and asked, "*Por favor*, Jennifer and Deena, would you work on the graves behind the theater where we found twenty bodies last year? I really think that there may be two more. Deke and I are assuming this, and I want to show you two likely spots, one more distinctive than the other. We can tell because the spot is like a stain in the rock—that is, the sediment is darker than the rock around it. *Por favor*, Jennifer, will you work on this more predominant stain? I think it may be a baby's grave because it is so small. *Gracias.*"

Deena worked on the less predominant stain. Since it was hard to know the difference between the dirt and the rock, Deke took a sprayer and sprayed the ground with water to show that the stain was actually dirt (darker color) while the lighter color was rock.

So I started to dig (more like scraping and brushing), and within two minutes I found two bones! It was surprising because they were so near the top. Deke was also surprised! He then explained that I needed to outline the grave, that is, to find the edges of the grave, because then I could dig within the edges once they were found. That was very frustrating and difficult because it was so hard to tell the difference between the rock and the dirt. Deke even commented on how undefined it was. So he started, and I took over. The best way to find the edges is to start where you know for sure it's rock then go in from there until, by the feel of the trowel, you can tell it's not as hard to dig, all the way around the edge. Due to my untrained eye and trowel skills, this was quite stressful; I didn't want to mess anything up. Sadly, Deke did not pick up the bones I had found and therefore when I was slowly moving around the edge, I accidentally sat on one of the bones and broke it! Oh my goodness—but it wasn't a big deal

I guess. Anyway, I got most of the edge done by break time.

After the break, Hernando brought a small plastic bag over to Deena for all the bones she had found and would find. He then took over and, to her excitement, found more bones.

As I watched Dr. Torres brushing the dirt away and shoveling it up, he made it look so easy, I enjoyed watching him work, with such skill and consistency. He not only found more bones but also some ceramic pottery pieces. He did his master's thesis on ceramic pieces, so with just a small fragment he could place the time period, which was the late Roman Empire. So this body was also buried during that time period, very interesting! He says it's better to find a body buried with other materials, because then it's easier to date. Hernando seems very kind. Even though he speaks mainly Spanish, he would make sure that he showed me all the pieces he found before putting them in the bag, and with the bones he would hold it up to his body to compare where he thought it came from. One of the pieces he thought could have been a piece of the jaw, shoulder, or hip. The pieces I found he thought may be part of the arm and the other one pelvis. He also commented that he thought that this person was not very well-liked because the bones were not consistent and were scattered all over the place, and the grave itself was not well-dug. It was just like in the movies: I was sitting there, brushing away dirt and discovering another bone. It was really exciting and nerve-wracking, because I didn't want to break another bone! (Deke broke one as well, though, so I was not the only one.) I keep feeling like I am in a movie just being here and walking through the villages and such. It's crazy!

I have yet to know why Hernando chose me, the youngest and least knowledgeable one of the group, but it was a blessing and thrilling to be able to experience that. I am not sure if I will continue the work Monday or we will be switching to other areas, but it was very neat!

Jennifer, in her area, also found some bones, although unlike Deena's, which were just fragments of bones, she was finding more of a complete body, and it looked to be a baby. Hernando's son was also digging a grave, and shortly, he had most of the skull uncovered. The other group members excavated more of the trench.

Part of the program included field trips to nearby historical and archaeological points of interest. So in the afternoon the team toured some Roman ruins in other towns. They visited two Roman-built bridges, a fifteenth-century castle, and a medieval (post-Roman era) Catholic Church. They were told that the stones used to build the church were stolen Roman gravestones and that looted or stolen stones from Clunia could be found all over in the surrounding villages. They also visited Pendorana Castle and church, from the sixteenth century. In the castle they climbed up in the tower, which had been renovated into a delightful museum. They also went into the Pendorana village square and visited the outside of the nobleman's palace, where a wedding was taking place.

Again, it was just like the movies: the little villages, with narrow, cobblestone streets and the old people sitting out in front of their houses. It was phenomenal just sitting there watching people drive or walk by. Sometimes there would be two of them or a group of them playing cards together. The houses were tall and all attached together with the iron "fences" on the windows (making a balcony) with brightly colored flower pots filled with equally brightly colored flowers in them. Everyone here dresses so nicely, women in dresses and men in slacks and button-up shirts. I find myself wishing James were here!

About 9:30 p.m. they went to a little bigger city, Tierra Aranda, for dinner, where they joined in a street fiesta until around midnight. By then, everyone was tired and ready to go home. On Sunday, another tour was scheduled, this time to Gumiel de Izán for a medieval festival.

Sunday, July 5, 2009

The festival was very interesting. The village square was all decorated for the medieval time period with flags and costumes. I felt like I was on the set of *Robin Hood*. There were little shops set up where you could buy jewelry, food, and such. As soon as we walked into the square, we were accosted by two guys dressed up as jokers or street jesters. One had a fur-covered club and the other had a long fur-covered stick with a fake hand on the end of it.

They were hitting people in the head and shoulders, or in my case, the guy with the club hit me on the top of the head while the guy with the fake hand stick thing hit me on my derriere! Ridiculous! It was not long until the shops closed down for the siesta. So we bought sandwiches from a bar and sat on the church steps to eat them in the shade.

At 4:00 p.m. the team went to see a Roman villa, with some preserved mosaics. Since there was no attendant, they looked around town to find someone to let them in. Finding no one, they went back to the Roman villa and just looked through the slits in the wooden fence to see the very beautiful mosaics. Then they returned to the village with the medieval festival, where the shops were open again, as was the church. They chose to go into the church, which was dark and emphasized Jesus' death, but not His resurrection.

When I returned to the flat, I decided I would call my former teacher, Teresa Martino. I was able to get her on the phone and invite her to come and see the dig. She said she was quite busy until the end of July but would try to make it over then because on July 25, she had to go to Madrid for a couple days. I hope that works out—I would love to have a really neat Christian girl with me for a day or two!

Anyway, I feel as though I am not only physically fighting for my health and rest but also spiritually fighting with all that goes on here, yet the Lord has shown me His mighty strength and peace, and I know His powerful and loving arms surround me. It's so reassuring to know that He is on my side, and will always fight for me and with me. What a joy it is to serve the Lord even in trials, condemnation, and temptations.

There is a praise item though: Sharon is feeling much better, and her grandfather is off life support. She is staying! I reminded her that the day she found out about her grandpa, I would ask people to pray for her. She laughed, but the Lord has answered our prayers! Oh, if she only knew how serious prayer is! (Mom, Hannah, even James, said they were praying.) I was reading my Bible last night, and she asked what I was reading. When I told her, she acted surprised and asked if I was Catholic. I told her "what I was," and she told me she was Catholic. Interesting.

Monday, July 6, 2009

Deena woke up feeling sick (with symptoms including runny nose, head all plugged up, ears ringing, fever), but still decided to go out to the site. At the site, Hernando asked Sharon to work with Deena on the grave she had been working on the day before. They worked for a while and found nothing—no more bones or pottery. He came by later and said, "*Por favor*, just clean up the area and cover the hole because I think everything has been found. I cannot be sure where these bones came from, since they are only fragments."

So after they scooped/shoveled up all the loose dirt and rocks, Hernando took them to another site. Once again the stain was hard to determine, yet they set to work on finding the edges of the grave. Deena was the one, now, who had to explain to Sharon how to do everything because it was her first time. Deena could relate to Sharon's frustration since she had gone though the same feeling of not knowing what she was doing.

As I was scraping I actually hit, causing a punctured hole in a human skull! I found not only one but two human skulls! It was rather thrilling! They were pretty close together, and as we kept trying to map out the edge of the grave, Hernando came over and was impressed and said that there may even be more remains in that one grave. He thought maybe a total of three or even four bodies. The grave we are digging is right beside another grave that was excavated last year.

After the break, about noon, Deena and Sharon were sent back to work on the mass grave, as it was called, as it was the talk of the site. Sophia and Deke both came over and started working with them, as did Jennifer. (Her baby's grave hadn't produced any artifacts. All the bones she found were fragments.) So there was quite a group working on the grave, scraping, digging, trying to determine the location of its edge, or border. Then Sophia found a third skull.

In the meantime, the Spanish archaeologist, Suzana, had dug a huge hole. Hernando didn't know what it could be at first. She had excavated down quite deep, and then she found a human body and also huge animal bones. Hernando commented, "Maybe this body was the chief or leader of the other bodies we have found, and he is with his horse! Some of the stains in the hole are from places where wood had been but is now rotted and disintegrated. It has been a very exciting and interesting day!"

> Deke sent me back to the house around 2:00 since my cold was still hanging on, and I was getting heat exhaustion. I fell asleep right away and didn't get up for lunch. I did get up around 4:00 and went to do e-mail. Just talking with my friends and family on Skype and Facebook makes me so thankful to hear their voices. After I finish this journal entry I will take a shower and then go to bed. I will not be going to dinner as I am trying to get rested up to get rid of this cold! God is good!

Tuesday, July 7, 2009

Deena spent most of Tuesday sleeping. She woke up feeling a little better but decided just to take it easy and stayed in her room the whole morning. At noon, Deke came by the flat to check the hot water and to check in on her. He left her a package of powdery stuff and said, "Mix it with a liter of water, and it will give a ton of nutrients to your body." She drank it as fast as she could, just to get it over and done with. It tasted terrible!

> The powdered drink must have made me feel better because I have washed the dishes and cleaned the bathroom! I tell you boys are dirty! Yikes! Something interesting about the village we are staying in: every hour on the hour and every half hour, an old church bell rings. For example, it just rang twelve times because

it's 12:00 noon, then it will ring once again at 12:30. It's kinda neat and it gives the feeling of being back in time. When Deke was here, I asked him how it was going down at the site. He said that more skeletons were being found, so that is interesting. I told Sharon to take pictures for me.

I really enjoyed just spending time by myself this morning. When the alarm clock woke me up, I told Sharon that I would not be going out. Shortly afterward, I fell back to sleep, but I woke up just a few minutes later and had such a sweet time with the Lord. I was able to pray—well, talk with him out loud. I prayed for loved ones. Also thanked Him for holding me in His arms during this time and for the reassurance that He is always with me, and that I also have two, if not more, huge, majestic, beautiful, powerful angels watching and on guard (which He made evident the night of the fiesta when I was in the back of the Jeep feeling completely and utterly alone). Wow, to be loved that much and to have that kind of army behind me, "whom/what shall I fear?" *Nothing!* The confidence we have in the Lord really truly surpasses all understanding, and to think that we can't even fathom all that He can do for us and through us if only we let Him. Also to think that what I am experiencing here outside of the archaeology site work is really not "that bad" and could always be much worse compared to so many things, yet He sees us through the small things, proving His much-deserved honor and praise. Although I am completely and utterly alone physically (as far as Christian fellowship), I *can more than overcome those around me spiritually! And that is something to be in awe of, something to praise the Lord for!*

By 2:30 p.m. everyone had returned from another day on the site. Sharon told Deena that they had found three sets of leg bones from the grave they were working on the day before (which apparently belonged to the skulls that were found). Sophia dug out more of the third skull and found the teeth—only the top ones. The jaw was missing. They named the bodies Larry, Moe, and Curly. It was another productive day, although Sharon said that she broke a kneecap and a fingernail as she was digging. She also mentioned that the next few times Hernando came over he asked, "So did you break anything else?"

At 3:00, Deena decided to go to lunch, even though she wasn't sure it was a good idea. Lunch consisted of green veggies, fish, and chocolate cake. She didn't eat much of any of it. (Everything seemed to be cooked in at least a pound of butter!) She didn't have much of an appetite anyway.

At midnight Deena woke up to Sharon throwing up in the bathroom, and again, every hour after that. It seemed like they were just switching spots: Sharon was sick, then Deena was sick, then Sharon again. At 6:30 the alarm went off, and Deena got ready for the day with her typical breakfast of muffin and juice. Sharon decided to stay home.

Wednesday, July 8, 2009

When Deena arrived at the site, she found out that the other girls on the second floor were also sick in the night, all three of them throwing up. Then when the few who were not sick arrived at the Spaniards' house, they found out that half of them had been sick during the night too.

Deena was paired up with Maria, one of the Spanish students, and was looking forward to working on Larry, Moe, and Curly, but instead worked with Maria on Body Number 25 (the name given to that skeleton). Maria and her usual partner had started uncovering Body Number 25 a few days earlier. Thankfully she spoke some English; actually, Deena felt she spoke it very well, even though Maria didn't think so.

"Maria, where did you learn your English?" Deena asked.

"I took English lessons from a teacher from London from when I was six until I was eighteen."

"How old are you now?"

"I am twenty-one and in my third year as a history major at a university here in Spain."

They worked well together, and it seemed that the day went by very fast. They uncovered most of the skull and face as well as many ribs and even some of the vertebrae. Both arms were uncovered folded in front of the body, but one of the hands was missing. Deena uncovered most of the pelvis and hip bones together with both femurs and the lower parts of both legs. All in all, they found the entire body (including teeth and jaw), except for one hand and both feet. Hernando thought that the one hand could have fallen below the hipbone because the arm was across the body and the end of the arm bone ended right at the hip. The feet could still be buried lower in the ground. They had to be so careful; the bones broke so easily. Plus, they needed to keep most of them in place, so that, once it was all uncovered, they could take a picture. Only after that could the bones be removed. When Hernando stopped by he said, "You are doing a very good job!"

"That's good to hear," the girls said together.

"This body, Number 25, as I call him or her, has a nice smile. I think that is because of the body's position and because the grave was so poorly made. It was probably too small for the body so that whoever buried it had to kick the body in to make it fit."

After Hernando left, Deena said to Maria, "Let me tell you—I think he looks rather gross. With the jaw wide open, it looks like a skull that would jump out on Indiana Jones!"

I find this work all very interesting. As I was brushing and scraping the dirt away from the face and skull, I could not help but wonder: Who are these people? What was their life like? What did they do, or what happened that they didn't get a proper burial? I actually felt very bad for this individual—two thousand years ago, he or she was thrown into the dirt—makes you wonder! As for Larry, Moe, and Curly, more of their bodies were uncovered. Larry's head/skull faces to the left, and so does Moe's as far as we can tell right now. He has more dirt covering him because he is in the middle. Then there is Curly. We all feel bad for him because his face is facing straight up, and by the looks of it (because of the bone formation) his face had been crushed, almost as if it had been smashed in with a huge rock or something. Whatever it was, it was not very pleasant. I feel I have a certain "right" to Larry, Moe, and Curly since I was the first one to find the skulls, but don't get me wrong; I am enjoying the site work, wherever I am placed. It was also nice to get to know Maria a little today. She seems very sweet; she often commented that she wished she was home, where there were clouds, as it was a hot day today. Another successful day, and praise the Lord, I am feeling much better. Now I just pray I will not get this flu that is going around!

I have more thoughts today. After e-mailing earlier and talking with Mom and friends (Hannah and James, yeah!) on Skype, I headed back to the flat and ended up reading for a bit and talking with Sharon. After I told her about e-mailing my mom, she wanted to go back to the Spaniards' house and e-mail her mom. She seems to be feeling a little better, but not much.

I was thinking more about Body Number 25 and Larry, Moe, and Curly. I often have wondered while digging up the bones of these bodies that have been buried for almost two thousand years. I wonder where they came from, why they died, why they were buried in such careless ways, and did they have family—were they married? As for Body Number 25, Hernando said that he/she was probably kicked and forced into the grave in order to make him/her fit because it was a small grave. It makes me sad. Twenty-five or more bodies have now been found. Could they have been persecuted Christians? Those who died for their faith, those who even through hardships, trials, condemnation and torture, and finally death still claimed their Lord and Savior as King—too good for this world! I think of Curly who had his/her face smashed in. Was he/she silenced because he/she was claiming Jesus as the Son of God? Oh, to have such faith! Maybe they are with the Lord, enjoying His glory and fellowship, singing His much deserved praise and worship. Of course these are just thoughts. We may never know, and their stories and lives will be a mystery forever. But we can hope they are with the Lord. Makes me wonder—if they were martyrs—would I be bold enough to go through the same fate as they did? I pray the Lord would give me the strength.

Thursday, July 9, 2009

Only three of the team—Luke, Sharon, and Deena—were well enough to be up at the site. No one else, not even Deke or Sophia, could make it. The three waited at the Spaniards' house for a while and only three of them were able to make it up. The flu seemed to be hanging on. Deena worked on Larry and Moe—Larry, in the morning till snack time, after which she cleaned off some of Moe—just getting more of their bones uncovered. Deena worked with Sharon early, then Jennifer came out later, around 9:00 a.m., and she also worked with them. At about noon Hernando erected a little shade fort for the girls with scaffolding and a few tarps. He was worried they were going to bake in the sun. It really helped. Deena was thankful for the shade.

The excavated bones were very brittle and broke very easily. Many bones were broken during the day—but only into smaller pieces—not all were completely crushed. Another grave was found, and Sophia's boyfriend, Juan, who had arrived that week for a visit and to help, continued to dig that grave out until a skull was revealed. Hernando commented, "This grave is actually a very well-made grave with huge rocks covering the sides and top. It is very deep, much deeper than those found earlier. I believe this grave was earlier than Larry, Moe, and Curly's grave, because more effort has been put into it, making it neater."

Friday, July 10, 2009

To my relief, everyone is better today and at the work site, except for Hernando's son. I started working on dusting more of the dirt off Larry, Moe, and Curly, and was working with Sharon, Luke, and Jennifer. We were getting the skeletons ready to take a picture for documentation. The others were telling me that they thought it was my calling in life to dig up graves and bones, since they all thought I did such a good job of it, better than any of them. I think the difference was that I actually cared about doing a good job, and by today they were pretty sick of digging up bones. Some were actually swearing and getting mad as they kept breaking bones. Anyway, we finally exposed as many of the bones as possible.

Then Hernando said, "I have to wait to take the picture until the sun is directly above or at least in a location where there will not be any shadows, so, *por favor,* go and start digging on the south side at the back of the theater, near the left side of Body Number 25. Someone spotted the telltale signs of a hole or a pit about three years ago, and the area has since been covered over. See if you can find it. *Gracias.*"

They began looking for this phantom hole. At noon Hernando

and Sophia showed the girls how to use the surveyor's level. First they needed to get it calibrated to the benchmark elevation (which happened to be a stone directly in the middle of the theater stage). They used it to compare the elevation of one of the gravesites on the south side of the theater, close to where they were trying to find the hole or pit (a stain in the rock). This was done with each gravesite for documentation, which made for a more accurate map. The main archaeologists also went around drawing or mapping out the whole area.

They then took a nice long snack break down at the Spaniards' house, where Hernando brought out wine, water, flat round bread, fruit, cheese, and meat. When snack time was over, they returned to learning to use the level. Sharon and Deena worked with Deke trying to find the hole. They were first told it was in a certain place, so Deke used the pickaxe while Sharon and Deena were on the shovels. Then it was not long before one of the Spaniards would say, "Oh wait—actually I think it's over there"—which was another five feet to the left. This went on for a while, moving every few feet. It made them feel like pirates digging for lost treasure without a map! They never found the hole, although they did dig up some bones and also some pottery.

While this was going on Jennifer was chosen to take the pictures of Larry, Moe, and Curly, and then she actually started to sketch them. Therefore, the team expected to start to carefully remove their bones the next day.

Suzana, the Spanish archaeologist who was digging the huge gravesite with the human skeleton and the animal skeleton on the north side of the back of the theater, thrilled the team with the discovery of a still-intact pottery bowl, with a coin in it! It was very exciting for her as well as for Hernando, since he would be able to better date the findings. She also found a ring—still on the finger! It was rather heavy, kind of bluish in color, but Deena could not see what was on the face of it because it was so dirty.

Saturday, July 11, 2009

At 8:00 a.m. everyone from the North American team was at the site for the first time in several days. Some were fortunate to be assigned to work on gingerly removing the bones of Larry, Moe, and Curly from their grave. Hernando picked Carla, an anthropology major, and Kayla, a biology major, as they would know the most about the bones, and the labeling would be done correctly. Then Jennifer and Sharon joined them to help out. Deena was assigned with the boys, Rick and Luke, and worked on trying to find another pit. There were actually three or four pits around the graves that appeared to have originally been used as storage areas. Again, Deena felt like she was just playing and throwing dirt around. Hernando came over and said a few things that she didn't understand, so she just followed the guys' lead since they understood Spanish. The guys continued digging for a while and then they decided that Hernando had actually said that they were supposed to sweep and clean the area, so Deena started to clean the area.

> Luke was like, "Actually I don't know what he wanted us to do. I kinda forget." Arrggh—boys are ridiculous sometimes!! So he went and got Deke (who was just sitting watching the girls dig up the bones, and

telling them riddles—again arrgghh boys!). Anyway, Deke came and just swept around a few times, and he found the pit! It was right under our feet the whole time! Anyway, it was exciting to know that a hole actually existed! We found the edge all the way around, and just like the grave holes, it's filled with dirt, the color of which is darker than the edge. Hernando came over and was pleased. We then had to measure the hole. So we measured the circumference and added the sketch of it to the other sketch of a hole nearby. Then I used the level again to find the elevation of the hole. I was starting to perspire, not because it was hot but because I had to do math, and math has never been my favorite subject. Unlike yesterday when I had to figure it out all on my own, I didn't want to mess it up, but thankfully I think all is good. Deke looked at it afterward and said it was fine! After that was done, we started digging up the hole, but we only got started when it was time to go. We have only found a few pieces of pottery and some animal bones so far.

Meanwhile, at Larry, Moe, and Curly's gravesite, the girls began digging up the bones, one at a time, wrapping each one in a kind of tissue paper and placing them in a bag. The bags of bones would be sent to a forensic anthropologist for analysis. The girls reached to about the pelvic area, working from the toes up. It was important to decide which body was put in the grave first, then second, and then third. It was decided that Moe (the one in the middle) was put in the grave first, since he was deeper and really squished by the other two. Then, maybe it was Curly, and finally, Larry. It would be nearly impossible to tell for sure. While the discussion was going on, Hernando mentioned, "This whole area of graves was like a butcher spot, since most of the bodies had something missing or cut off, such as heads, arms, legs, or hands. For example, one of Larry's hands was found under his pelvis, which means that it had been cut off and thrown in the grave before his body.

"About the grave site that Suzana is working on, the one that was thought to have the human remains and the animal remains, well, it turns out that the human remains are a child. The body didn't have any legs, which may have been cut off, and also it looks as though he/she had an elongated head. The little body was buried beside an animal we think is a dog. Also buried there was an egg. One of my colleagues looked up Roman rituals and found that it was a common ritual to bury a child with an animal and an egg and that these types of graves have been found all along the Mediterranean. We also found in that area another human skeleton, an adult body. The bones show his hands are up over his face, like he was trying to protect his face. We feel like he was put into the grave alive and then his face was smashed in with a rock and he had been trying to protect himself. You remember that this is the body that Suzana found with the ring on his finger. She also found that clay pot with the coin in it. I think that the coin was from the first or second century because the edges of the coin are very thick, and it's very big."

Deke then added, "I received the results from last year's findings, concerning the twenty bodies found, and it was discovered that most of them were men between the ages of twenty and forty. Also, they had unusually elongated heads."

Sunday, July 12, 2009

Another day of sightseeing. The first stop, after a two-hour trip, was the Visigothic church Santa Maria de Lara. Of only about a dozen Visigothic churches still standing, this one was the best preserved. The Germanic Visigoths had a short reign when they took over from the Romans in the fifth century. They were Arian Christians—that is, they did not believe in the Trinity—but soon converted to Catholicism. The Franks drove them out around AD 507.

Their second stop was the prehistoric Dolmen de Mazariegos, from about 3000 BC. The edifice, built with huge stones, looked like a grave igloo—a place where the people who lived there at that time would put their dead.

The third stop was Covarrubias, a village holding a medieval festival. As part of the festivities, some of the team had their picture taken posing as though they were getting their heads chopped off. This village, populated since pre-Roman days, was the home of Fernando Gonzalez who fought to gain control over the Muslims and began the foundation of Christian Castilla. In this village was the Gothic Colegiata Church, which the team toured, and was the burial place of a thirteenth-century Norwegian Princess, Kristina, as well as the tombs of Fernando Gonzalez and his wife Sancha.

The fourth stop was the Monastery of San Pedro de Arlanza. This monastery was built by Gonzalez's father in AD 912. In 1080 construction began to convert the original structure into a large Romanesque church, and the differences were apparent. Some windows were Gothic, some Roman. The team climbed the spiral rock staircase of the tower, which everyone thought was "very cool." Deena felt like she was back in time, like a princess climbing up to her chamber! Restoration of the monastery began in 2003.

It was a good day, long and tedious, but interesting and very neat! A few of us took a walk around the village while we were there. We walked across a river on rocks that were placed all across the river. Kinda fun!

A few days ago, I heard some bells in the distance, like cow bells. I was digging at the time, and I looked up and there on one of the gravel roads was a sheep herder (shepherd), with a flock of sheep; the bells were coming from the sheep, I guess. The sheep herder even had a staff—it was a great picture. I was thankful the Lord allowed me to look up when I did in order to see that picture. He will take care of His flock! I saw shepherds again today on our way out for our excursion.

Monday, July 13, 2009

Out on site, the girls continued to gently remove the bones of Larry, Moe, and Curly, while Deena continued to work with Luke and Rick on the hole. They found more haphazardly buried bones and pottery, some of which had figures etched, as though stamped, in the pottery. They found two large pieces which fit together, as well as two other pieces of the same type of pottery. They continued to the bottom of the pit. It was decided that the hole had been used for storage, so a sample of the dirt was taken from the bottom of the hole and sent to be analyzed to learn more about what had been stored there.

Then Dr. Hernando lectured spontaneously about the pottery. Looking at a piece in his hand he said, "This was made between AD 70 and 120. The figure on this pottery was Eros, otherwise known as Cupid, the god of love. It looks as though Eros was going toward vines or pine trees, which would have been the opening of a temple. It's called *Terra Stigillata* stamped pottery. As you can see, the stamp is on the bottom. It is a piece of luxury pottery and part of a huge cup—all the pieces with the stamped figures on them are part of the cup. Because it was luxury pottery—meaning, used for special occasions—the person who owned it would scratch his name in it for ownership reasons, and you can see one initial scratched into it, an 'A'. Since we have found many pieces, they are actually each a part of a 'set' of pottery, like our dinner sets of today. It is very rare for a whole set to be found together in one location like we found! Since we know the date of the pottery we can date the hole, and I would say it was dug at the end of the first century AD. The hole was dug after the construction of the theater, and they filled it near the end of the first century. It is my opinion that this hole is the first 'for sure' thing we have been able to date, due to the pottery found. I am very happy! *Muy bueno!*

"From the architectural point of view, that is, the architecture used in the construction, the theater people think that it's from the Tiberius Period. However, from the archaeological point of view, because of the artifacts that have been found, such as the pottery, it's proof that it's from the Mission Period. I believe it's more accurate to date from the archaeological point of view rather than the architectural point of view. I have been finding evidence for the past six years to prove the Mission Period dating is accurate."

•

After his lecture, Hernando took Sophia, Luke, and me to the front of the theater and pulled out the little note pad that he always uses to draw to show what he is trying to explain. (He also includes some sound effects.) So while we were standing in the arena part of the theater, he said, "I think that so far, after all of the digs we have had, that we are at the arena ground level. I also think that the bodies that are found here were people who had died during the gladiatorial games that were held here because they were all brutally killed and in pieces."

Sophia argued, "It could not be possible because the Romans did not bury their dead like that. They cremated them."

He replied, "When the Visigoths invaded they carried on with the games, so it could have been during their time. Also, if it were during the time of the Romans, they probably did not give those who died during the games the ceremonial burial of cremation anyway, since most were slaves and others of similar status."

Luke took up Sophia's side of the discussion. "It could not be gladiatorial bodies since there were some women and children's bodies found."

"The Romans were brutal to their slaves, who were probably Christians as well, and they didn't care; they would kill women and children, have them in the games as well," Hernando countered. (It reminded me of *The Mark of the Lion* books again!) I find it very interesting and informative listening to Hernando talk even though I don't understand the Spanish. You just know that he is full of information and insights. Plus, he makes it easy to understand with his little sketches and such, plus sound effects. He also is always making fun of something, in a teasing and harmless way.

After cleaning up and resting, the team headed over to the house for dinner. It was a good dinner with birthday cake for Sharon for dessert.

Tuesday, July 14, 2009

On site, the girls went back to cautiously extracting the bones of Larry, Moe, and Curly, while Deena was sent to a stain which was found near Suzana's huge hole, the one where the ring and child and adult skeletons had been found.

Again I had to find the edge and then dig it out. I found only one random bone and a few small pieces of pottery. The grave was only about a meter long, 30 cm wide and 10 cm. deep. Once that was done, I was sent to help Rick and a new visitor/team member named Mark who were working on digging out another pit found on the other side of Suzana's huge hole. I was using the trowel most of the morning while Mark shoveled and Rick pickaxed. It was interesting getting to know Mark. He is in his late 30s, from the U.K., so he has a strong British accent. He is a communication teacher from Oxford but also a freelance writer. He proposed to write an article on archaeology for *The Guardian* newspaper. They liked the idea and sent him here to do his research. He will be here for about a week and will be writing his article about this dig.

After the break, Deke switched Mark and Rick with Carla and Kayla, who went to dig out the bones, and Mark and Rick joined Deena digging in the pit. Deena worked the pickaxe all the rest of the afternoon. In the pit they found some random cow bones, pieces of pottery, and pieces of column. The dirt in this pit was much different than the one they had been working on previously. It was very soft, rich, and dark. The pit was also much deeper than the other one, and the bottom had not been reached by the end of the workday.

Chapter 10

Discovery—Wednesday, July 15, 2009

On site at 7:00 a.m., Sharon and Mark finished taking out the bones of Larry, Moe, and Curly. As soon as Sharon removed Larry's skull, she called Deena over and they took pictures with the skull since Sharon and Deena were the ones who originally found them. When all the bones were out and marked, it was obvious that the grave they were in went down deeper, so Deena asked if she could go down and look for what else might be there.

"Good idea, Deena. Keep us posted."

She had been there only a few minutes when she exclaimed, "Look at this; I think it is some sort of metal object!"

"Carefully lift it out, Deena, and see what it is."

"It looks like a tube—maybe it is copper. Could that be?"

"Hand it up. Let's have a look."

Deke, Jennifer and Rick were working on a trench in the stage area of the theater, taking out more columns, but they hurried over to see what all the excitement was about.

"Look what Deena found in the bottom of the grave."

"It looks like a copper tube. Do you suppose there is something inside it?"

Just then Hernando came over and exclaimed, "We are

certainly fortunate! Another first for this dig! I think we better send it to the forensic lab. Good going, Deena!"

"All right, everybody, let's go back to work."

Luke, as on Tuesday, was working with Suzana and her crew of Spaniards on her huge hole. Deena continued working with Carla and Kayla on the hole they had been digging out the previous day. But the talk in every area was the wonder of what might be the meaning of the discovery of a copper tube and how long it might be before they would know what it was.

After we took pictures of Larry, Moe, and Curly, I asked if I could check the bottom of the grave, and I found what looked like a copper tube. No one seems to know what it could be, so it's going to the lab!

Back at the other pit, we were supposed to be looking for the different layers. Well, we didn't know where one layer started and one ended—the dirt looked the same to me—so we kept digging. Anyway, I was pretty frustrated by break time, yet we did happen to find a piece of mosaic, so Hernando was pretty impressed with that. It was after break that things actually got fun. Hernando was pleased. "Deena, would you measure and sketch this excavation?"

The problem was that neither of the other girls had done it before, and I had never done the sketching before. Thankfully, Hernando is very patient. He assigned me to the sketching, so more math! Since I had to use grid paper and draw it to scale, at least I remembered what the "y" axis was and what the "x" axis was. So now I have officially done every job possible when measuring an area: reading the level, holding the measuring level rod, measuring the length and width of hole. And actually, sketching was the most fun of all once I got the scale down. It was helpful to have Hernando around.

Once that was done, Hernando told us to keep digging deeper. So the rest of the time we just rotated getting into the pit and filling buckets up with dirt and passing them out. To make the time go by faster, we told riddles and played Twenty Questions and "Add On to the Story," where we each add a sentence at a time to a story. There were lots of laughs, and the afternoon did go by pretty fast. It was nice working with those girls. Now that the awkward just-getting-to-know-each-other stuff is out of the way, we are able to have more fun.

Amazing as it may sound, I am really excited about the tube I found this morning. What could be inside? Could it be something that would change the way people think about this site and what actually happened here? And when will we know?

Thursday, July 16, 2009

Sharon and Mark continued on the hole beneath Larry, Moe, and Curly's grave, but they didn't come up with anything else. They then spent time sweeping off the entire grave area, getting it ready for more pictures. Deke, Rick, and Jennifer continued to work on the trench they had started in the middle of center stage in the theater. Luke continued to work in the huge hole helping the Spaniards. Once that was done, he helped sweep the area. Carla,

Kayla, and Deena worked on the hole they had been working on previously. Deena was pickaxing, and about the fifth time down the hole, she noticed that the color of the dirt changed. It was not as dark and was rockier. So Hernando was called over and he told them they were doing a good job and that the excavation was complete, all the way to the bottom (about 1.5 meters deep.) "*Por favor,* do another sketch of the final hole." Deena did the sketch again, while the others found and read off the measurements. Since it was the bottom of the hole, they also had to measure and sketch the depth of the hole for a side view. So Kayla drew while Carla and Deena took the measurements. They finished right before break time.

During the break, talk was again about the possibility of a momentous find. What, if anything, was inside the tube, and when would they be able to find out? Hernando did not know but promised to check again with the lab.

Deena then joined the Spanish students down at the house—in the makeshift garage lab—washing the pieces of column that had been found so far. There were many pieces. Simply using buckets filled with soap and water, they scrubbed them clean. When they finished washing all of the pieces that were by the house, they remembered there were several more pieces down by the lower gate, so the girls went down, retrieved those pieces, and started cleaning them. Deena was thankful when it was time to go back to the flat; it had seemed like a long day.

Friday, July 17, 2009

Finished with the grave of Larry, Moe, and Curly, the girls were sent back to the inside of the theater where the team first started.

Three older Spanish men had been working on the trench area on the south side of the theater—the same area where the team started the first few days. The three Spanish men had done a lot of work. Then Deke asked for a volunteer to offer to go and work with them. No one did, so Deena finally offered. Luke also joined, as well as two other female Spanish students. The three men didn't usually show up until 8:00, so the four team members worked on their own until they arrived. The three men had a rather good system since they had been doing this kind of work for many years, and it seemed possible that the team actually slowed them down.

> The "Tres Amigos," as we call them, are very kind. There is one, Saul, who I think is more likeable than the others. He is a short ball of bone and muscle. His hands, arms, and face are work-and-sun-worn, and the wrinkles on his face are almost as deep as those on the face of a pug pup, which made his quick and easy smile stand out even more! All three have a mixture of tobacco and wine thick on their breath. Their "hydration" is a bottle of wine they keep hidden yet easily accessible.

It was cloudy and cool, and the wind kept up in the afternoon, so even with the sun out, it was cool at the site. Deena did a lot of shoveling and wheelbarrowing, but left the pickaxing to the professionals. The men filled the wheelbarrow up with dirt, and Deena wheeled it over to a plank set up to the lip of a Bobcat-type machine with a big scoop and dumped the dirt in. This meant she had to push the heavy wheelbarrow full of dirt and balance it up the narrow plank. It was a little tricky at first, but she soon got the hang of it. Deena appreciated the compliment from Hernando, "You are very strong and handle the wheelbarrow very well."

They found lots of pieces of columns, some very small, others very large. Hernando explained, "Looters would come and make off with the huge support blocks from the bottom, knocking down the surrounding parts. Then, obviously over time, without the support, the large columns would fall, leaving the big pieces of column to fall where they might. From where they fell, and which layer of dirt they are in, I can reasonably determine the date of the construction and the destruction."

Jennifer and Rick continued to work on the front stage area, while the others were working on the cliff above the theater, where they could look down into the theater.

> The Tres Amigos left early, so we four team members continued without them and then were sent to the garage lab to wash more columns. It was nice sitting in the sun where it was warmer. I enjoyed today much more than yesterday. I feel I accomplished much more. Still no word on the contents of the copper tube.

Saturday, July 18, 2009

It was another full day of tourist activities for the team. At 10:30, they left for the Roman City of Tiernes (Soria). Deke had done his first dig in this city in 1996. Sophia also had done some digging at this site. Unfortunately, digging had stopped due to political reasons. Foundations could still be seen carved into the bedrock. Using tools very similar to those of today, such as levels and theodolites, Roman engineers calculated the exact slope to keep the water running through the aqueduct for twenty-four hours a day. The aqueduct was also carved into the bedrock. Walking through the tunnel of the aqueduct, the team said it was a little scary because it was so dark, "but really neat!"

After lunch they went to Caracena Castle, built in the fifteenth century. The team enjoyed just being able to explore, since they were the only visitors there. They climbed up and walked along the wall, about thirty feet up—also a little scary, because it was so windy. Many took group pictures, exclaiming it was easy to imagine what life was like back in that day, with knights, kings, and queens.

The next stop was Gormaz Castle, the largest fortress by surface area (1,200 square meters) in Europe. A Muslim stronghold, it was never conquered by the Christians, because in the tenth century, the fortress boasted quite a large population.

> Gormaz Castle was huge! It was amazing, built on the top of a high plateau, and it took up the whole plateau! The scenery was breathtaking, and you could see for miles! There was a river nearby, just so beautiful. I was praising God for his amazing creation almost the whole time. I climbed up into the highest tower, a little difficult (only a few of us attempted this), but it was worth it! It was awesome! We saw a few churches along the way but didn't stop as they were Romanesque. While just driving through the countryside, you see a ton of ruins. My thoughts were always going back in time.
>
> We stopped for lunch at a bar nearby. The bar gave free shots of their house liquor. I didn't have any, and most everyone could not finish theirs because it

was so strong. Rick finished the bottle and had beer and wine on top of that. He admits he is an alcoholic and seems proud of it. Lord, help me to be a "river of life" flowing out to him!

Sunday, July 19, 2009

Another day of touring, so at 12:00 noon, we left for the medieval town of Lerma. Once there, we were given maps from the tourist place, and Sharon, Carla, and I just walked around and went to all the areas labeled on the map. We saw arches, churches, and more churches, but the most impressive was the palace. The palace is now a very beautiful hotel. We went inside, and it was amazing—with huge rock columns, marble floors—just really neat. We had lunch there in Lerma at a bar. Then we came back to the flat. I was really tired so I took a nap.

At 8:30, I read Romans 15 and got excited because Paul was talking about going to Spain! It made things real, a lot of "what ifs," such as, what if he was really here, in this theater? Then reading Romans 16:1-2, talking about Phoebe, I wondered if she was ever here. It was exciting because it brought to light everything that I am doing here! Just praying the Lord is in it all, and that He will bless it and be glorified! I was so excited about it that I told Sharon, but she didn't really understand and was not nearly as excited. Lord, work in Sharon's heart to show her your love and the abundant life.

Monday, July 20, 2009

Monday morning when Hernando arrived, he called everyone over. "I called the laboratory this morning," he announced. "They opened the copper tube. It contained a rolled-up document. The document appears to be written in Greek on papyrus. You may know that papyrus is a hard, smooth medium, and ink does not soak into it. Therefore, it is very tricky to unroll the document without the old ink scaling off. I asked the lab what they intended to do about that. They said they have a process which would rejuvenate the papyrus and make it easier to unroll without losing the ink. Then I asked how long it would take. They thought that it may take a week or two. I told them we would really appreciate some idea of what was written on the papyrus before the end of the month, if possible. They told me to call again next Monday. They also said the roll appeared to be in codex form, that is, individual sheets, rolled up like a scroll. They think it was rolled up so it would fit into the copper tube and be sealed. Maybe we will know more next week. They did promise that if the sheets unrolled as envisioned, they will make copies for my university and anyone else who would like one. If it is in Greek as they suppose, someone will need to translate it for us or for whoever gets a copy. Yes, Deena?"

"Do you think I could have a copy, whether or not they get it unrolled before we leave?"

"Yes, I'm sure we can get a copy of whatever is there for you."

Hernando's announcement caused quite a buzz among the team, and it was difficult for Deena to begin working on the trench again with Luke and the two Spanish girls. At 8:00 when the Tres Amigos arrived, Deena was busy shoveling and wheelbarrowing again. It was a good place to work, since once the Bobcat was filled, work stopped while one of the men dumped it. Again they found many pieces of columns and capitals. Deena also was the first one to find a rock with paint on it, and soon everyone was looking and discovering several pieces in one area. Hernando was noticeably excited. As Deke said, "If you see his mustache dancing, you know he is happy."

> Today I noticed a cross that was made and moved by one of the Spaniards, and it was set up against one of the façades of the theater. I saw it every time I went by with the wheelbarrow, again an awesome reminder. It made me smile. It seems the Lord likes to continue to remind me that He is always with me!

Later in the day, after the Tres Amigos left, Deena was both shoveling and wheelbarrowing all the dirt into the Bobcat, walking on the plank, and dumping the loads. Hernando came by and talked to the Spanish girls because he wanted some girls to go to the lab and do inventory. Suzana, the Spanish archaeologist, was working in the lab, which was similar to a school science lab: sinks, tall tables full of artifacts, chemicals, and scientific containers. She took the girls to the garage (also set up as a makeshift lab) and there explained what to do: Label all the pieces of columns and capitals that had been collected so far, by taking old fountain pens, dipping them into the ink, and in very small print, writing the year, a number, and a letter, so it would look like this: *09 22/147 D.*

I finished reading Romans today. Paul really wanted to come to Spain. Could he have been here? Being here brings the book of Romans to life and makes it even more real, and I feel part of history!

Tuesday July 21, 2009

Tuesday morning, Deena went with Delia, a Spanish student, to the garage lab and started labeling the artifacts (pieces of columns) with the fountain pen. Before writing, they had to paint the area they were going to write on the rock artifact with a special clear substance, because the substance made the ink soak in better. They took the pens, dipped them in ink, and started writing. When the pieces were all labeled, a chart of all the artifacts had to be made. One column was for the label number just written on all the artifacts, the second column was for the description of the piece. The description included what part of the column the piece was, such as the base (bottom), column (middle), or capital (top), including its measurement, the height, width, and length. Since Deena could not write in Spanish, Delia wrote while Deena measured.

At 11:00 the acting US Ambassador and his wife, along with his secretary, her husband, and an intern came to visit the theater. Team members were warned to be on their best behavior, and since Deena was down in the lab she didn't see much of them. But because they were very special visitors, Deena and Delia left work early to go to lunch with them. Deena wore her new white Spanish celebration blouse tucked into white pants with a brightly colored waistband and tan sandals. They all went to lunch at the city of Penaradoa and ate at the most fancy restaurant called La Posada Ducal.

> We were at the restaurant for a long time. The view out of the restaurant window was overlooking the castle, and it was awesome, just like olden times! The food was great! I was asked to sit beside the ambassador and his wife. His wife was very kind; she was from Honduras and I enjoyed my nice talk with her. Rick had my wine and shot since I wasn't going to drink it, and Sophia had enough wine for at least three of us. The secretary's husband also enjoyed the alcohol, so we had a few who were feeling pretty good by the time we finally got out of there.

Wednesday, July 22, 2009

The next few days were rather anticlimactic and routine as the crew waited for the news from the lab about the document in the copper tube. Back in the garage lab, Deena and Delia worked all morning finishing the labeling and charting of the artifacts the team had found. Then they photographed all of the artifacts. Both of the girls learned how relic photographs were taken and appreciated the opportunity.

In the afternoon they went to the pool in Huerta, the small village where the team usually ate most of their meals. It was quite a nice pool, together with a kiddie pool, snack counter, and, of course, a bar. Luke, Jennifer, Sharon, Carla, and Deena had a nice time there, but since only Jennifer actually brought a swimsuit, the rest of the girls went in shorts and tank tops. The water was very cold, yet refreshing, and they relaxed, read, and played cards.

> We were in the newspaper today because of the ambassador's visit, with pictures of the theater and such. I think they are going to try to get us all copies. I want to mention about a dog Jennifer has named Tick (due to the fact we were told he had ticks). He is an obnoxious dog that waits for us almost every morning at the top of the hill we climb on the way to the Spanish house. He jumps up on us—he especially likes Jennifer—kinda funny. The sunflowers are out and blooming, fields and fields of them—very pretty!
>
> I guess we won't hear anything more from the lab until Monday. The wait and the mystery are making me anxious.

Thursday, July 23, 2009

It was raining early in the morning, so everyone went back to bed. Deena was thankful for the extra few hours of sleep. At 10:00, she woke up and returned to the house where she worked in the garage lab again, taking pictures of artifacts all by herself. She accomplished quite a bit, but then the camera battery ran out, so she went back to labeling more artifacts. As for the others and their work on the site, Luke was still with the Tres Amigos working on the trench area. The group that was working at the front of the theater, digging for the floor of the theater, had reached it and then cleaned it up. Sharon and Carla continued digging at the top of the theater.

A tour bus was out at the site today, taking lots of pictures of the team working. Seems funny being on the other side of the pictures. So many tourists who have been through will take candid pictures of us working—weird. I'm so excited about the document in the tube and what it could mean—can hardly wait! But I did get a copy of the newspaper clipping from yesterday about the ambassador's visit—good keepsake!

Friday, July 24, 2009

Deena started out the morning back in the trench for about five minutes but then was moved back down to the lab to help label more artifacts since Delia was sick. As soon as they were labeled, she washed a few more pieces, then went back to the trench. She had not been at the trench for another five minutes before she was sent up to help at the top of the theater. Since she had not yet worked up there, Deena looked forward to finding out what was going on. When she arrived, she noticed that some rock and mortar were showing, so for the rest of the time, she just helped scrape off the dirt to reveal more of the rock and mortar. It turned out that the place they were scraping was the original main entrance to the theater!

So that's pretty interesting, finding the main entrance. It was a very cold, windy day today, but it was a good day. After digging, a posed picture was taken. Now Deke wants to take mock photos of famous photos. So, for example, today we took one of Neil

Armstrong climbing on the moon. It's hard to explain, but it actually looked pretty good. Anyway, who knows what the next one will be? Will it have something to do with the document in the tube?

Saturday, July 25, 2009

Deena worked all day labeling the artifacts. She found that she was becoming quite proficient with the fountain pen. And yet, there were so many items that she could hardly keep up, and Luke and Sharon were washing even more. Sharon brought her iPod and speakers to the lab, so they listened to music the whole time. This was a welcome diversion, as it made the time go by faster. The sun was very hot.

The others—Carla, Jennifer, and Rick—were working on the cliff, or top of the theater, where Deena had worked the day before. Kayla enjoyed working with a visiting professor, a man with a PhD who was at the site, examining and assessing the bones that Juan, Sophia's boyfriend, had dug up. By looking at the pelvis, forehead, and jaw, he concluded that it was a female, because the forehead and jaw of a male are flatter than that of a female. The skull had a bash in it, which, according to the doctor, was pre-death because it was on the verge of healing, but he didn't think it was necessarily the cause of death. The day went by quickly for Deena and the team.

At 5:00 p.m. the team went on another excursion to Necrópolis del Alto Arlanza, a town about an hour away. It was amazing how much the landscape changed going from farmland and fields to pine-covered hills and mountains.

When we were walking to the necropolis, an ancient city cemetery, it was as if I was back in Indiana, with the smell of pine trees and everything. It was great! At this necropolis there are about 183 graves carved into the rock, from medieval times, dating back to the ninth to thirteenth centuries. We noted both adult and infant size graves—many infant graves, since the mortality rate of infants was very high. Some graves were carved into the sides of rock cliff as well as the rock surface. After the necropolis, on our way back to the flat, we visited a dinosaur museum; apparently some dinosaur bones have been discovered in the area.

Sunday, July 26, 2009

My personal church service today was reading Titus. Actually, I really enjoyed it. Key verses are Titus 3:4-8. They reinforced the guidance the Lord has been giving me, to live as He would have me live, to glorify Him and by this show how the gospel is so beneficial.

I also wrote an e-mail to James asking him to come and see me in Indiana when I get back. I miss him so much!

At 12:30, the team left for Burgos, the largest city around and the capital of the province. There, they visited the Burgos Cathedral, which had beautiful architecture. It was huge! As with all of the churches visited, Deena felt rather depressed. It was a little eerie, and the smell and the music put things almost over the top. She felt the builders had expended so much effort into all the carvings and decorations, and so much emphasis on the death of Christ, but there seemed to be no reflection or joy expressed in His resurrection—so empty of what was truly important.

Next, they visited the working monastery, Cartuja de Miraflores. The team was given free time. While others went to a bar, Sharon and Deena visited the Burgos Castle. It was a very hot day, in the nineties. Since it was Sunday, nothing else was open, but they enjoyed just being outside and walking around.

Monday, July 27, 2009

Dr. Hernando again called the group together early Monday morning, and everyone cheered when he said, "The lab was able to unroll the document found in the copper tube. We are extremely fortunate that almost all the letters, such as, *alpha, beta, gamma*, etc., are recognizable, that is, not all the ink has flaked off. However, the words are the common Greek of New Testament times and not modern Greek. I have a colleague at the university who is a Greek scholar, and he will translate it into Spanish but not English. So I have contacted my friend, the president of the Biblical Archaeology Society, Hershel Shanks, and he said he would have one of his contributors translate it into English. Yes, Deena?"

"My New Testament professor could also do it for us."

"Yes, I'm sure there are many in the United States who could do the job. That is why I have a copy in the Greek for you and for anyone else who would like to have one."

Almost everyone raised their hands indicating they wanted a copy. Deena was pleasantly surprised that both Sharon and Rick asked for copies.

"There are a couple items that Dr. Carlos Molina, the Greek scholar, pointed out to me and may be of interest for those who have some familiarity with the New Testament. The document is a letter, dated the tenth year of the reign of Nero, about AD 65, from a woman, named Phoebe, and written to a man she called the apostle Paul." Deena's jaw dropped open. "Many will remember Paul as the author of several books in the New Testament. But Phoebe is mentioned only once, as far as I know, in the sixteenth chapter of Paul's letter to the Romans, where he asks his friends in Rome to make Phoebe welcome because she had tenderly helped many including Paul himself.

"One other thing is quite startling. It appears that she gives her full name as Salome Phoebe. Since my colleagues and I do not understand the Greek of the New Testament era, we do not yet understand the implications of this revelation. However, the fact that we found it under Moe's body seems to indicate that perhaps Moe is really Paul the apostle. We also know, from Romans 16, that Paul was interested in coming to Spain. From this evidence, we may be able to justify the proposition that he actually did arrive! What are the implications of this with regard to how he died? It certainly appears that Paul was killed here in this amphitheater and subsequently buried with two others who may have been his colleagues. We do know that Paul provoked trouble in many places he visited and therefore could have drawn attention to himself with his forceful preaching of Christianity. With these questions to consider, let's all go back to work!"

The small group was too astonished to move. Finally, Sharon approached Deena unobtrusively and asked, "Deena, you mentioned something about this the other night in our room. What made you think about it then?"

"The subject came up as I was reading Romans again. We studied this Scripture in New Testament Survey last semester and the prof talked about the possibility of Paul's going to Spain. Why do you ask?"

"I think I'd better look at the Bible again, because I had no idea that things like this really happened!"

"You know, I am feeling the same way, Deena," Rick interjected. "Please pray for me. I really don't feel good enough to know God personally."

Deena went back to the lab labeling more artifacts. She soon caught up to those who were washing. Since she could not write the labels on the artifacts when they were wet, she just helped those who were washing. Also, the Spanish students had already left, so it was just the Spanish archaeologists and a few of the American team members.

The other team members went to work up on the cliff (overlooking the theater) still clearing the area at the entrance of the theater. After snack time, Hernando came and talked with Luke, who, because he had hurt his wrist, was washing artifacts with Sharon and Deena. Hernando teased Luke and the way he was washing the pieces, being *so* sensitive to his wrist. The girls grinned. Hernando suggested that Luke should go for a walk to a Roman tower about a half hour's walk away, explaining that this was a possible future archaeological site, since beside the tower is a necropolis. The tower was in the middle of a farmer's field. Luke encouraged Sharon and Deena to walk to the tower with him, which, at one time, had been covered with decorative stones. Deena said that the tower reminded her of the water tower at her high school. The upper part of the tower was missing, so they climbed as far as they could and sat there for a while, talking about the letter found in the copper tube and wondering what it all meant. It was nice and relaxing, with a great view. They went back to the lab soon afterwards, washed a few more artifacts, and then were done for the day.

> Today was a monumental day for me. Since we learned that the letter was an instrument that may change the way historians think about how the book of Acts should end, I feel overwhelmed. But even more stirring are the exciting responses of Sharon and Rick. Dear Lord, do a work in their lives this week. Help me to know what to say to them.

Tuesday, July 28, 2009

At 7:00 a.m., back on the site, Deena was thrilled to be assigned to work at the trench with Rick and Carla—and of course the Tres Amigos. She spent all day wheelbarrowing and walking the plank. When she asked Rick to ask the Tres Amigos if she could get a picture of them, Saul, the boss, got excited and exclaimed, "Hey guys, we are going to America, in a picture." They made sure they had props (equipment) for the picture. It was funny, and then they wanted another picture for good time's sake. Deena enjoyed working on the site as she felt very productive, and the

Tres Amigos made work quite easy, since so much work was accomplished when they were around.

> Tonight after dinner we had a mini fiesta in our flat. It's Kayla's last night. She is leaving tomorrow, and then they are planning a big fiesta tomorrow night because it's everyone's last night.

Wednesday, July 29, 2009

Deena worked in the trench all day again with the Tres Amigos. She had a great day wheelbarrowing and received a nice compliment from her favorite "amigo," Saul. Directing the comment to Rick, so that he could translate, he said, "She works very hard—just like a Spaniard." Deena thought it was funny and that Saul was very sweet. He always made sure that the others didn't overfill the wheelbarrow so that Deena would be able to push it and get it on the plank, which was higher than usual. Hernando was also at the site, so Deena took a picture of him with Carla and Sharon. Saul let Carla and Deena sit on his Bobcat for pictures. He actually offered, surprising Deena, because he never let anyone drive his Bobcat; in fact, he was the only one that knew how to drive it. Finally, when they continued their work, they found the floor of the theater on the far side of the trench.

Kayla left the project early in the morning, and everyone missed her random and occasionally awkward comments. "She was sweet," they agreed.

> It's a bittersweet feeling today—sweet because I get to go home tomorrow to loved ones, who have been

very missed. Sweet also because I have cherished memories and a once-in-a-lifetime experience. Sweet because Teresa Martino came today. She helped me when I introduced her to the Tres Amigos. The bitterness is that this once-in-a-lifetime experience has now come to an end. I will miss going back in time (over two thousand years) every day as soon as I set my feet on the site. I will miss all the new discoveries each and every day. I will miss Hernando and his mustache, and his silly grin and sound effects. I will miss the beautiful weather and landscape. I will also miss those I have come to know here, knowing that I may never see them again. It breaks my heart that each one is still lost and in need of God's love. I hope and pray that by the grace of God that I will see them someday again in heaven. And I of course will miss the Tres Amigos, who brought a smile to my face every time I worked with them. Today, with Teresa's help, I gave Saul a New Testament in Spanish with these words on the flyleaf:

Dios Te Ama Juan 3:16 (página 166), Romanos 5:8 (página 275)

Todos Somos Pecadores Romanos 3:23 (página 272), Romanos 3:10 (página 272)

El Remédio de Dios para el Pecado Romanos 6:23 (página 277), Juan 1:12 (página 162), I Cor 15:3,4 (página 314)

<u>*Todos Pueden Ser Salvos*</u> Apocalipsis 3:20 (página 442), Romanos 10:13 (página 283)

At 7:00, we took one last walk of Clunia and the theater. I will miss it. At 8:00, we went to Huerta for a buggy ride; it was really fun and relaxing, saw the whole town. At 9:00, we ate dinner at the restaurant we had eaten at every day since being here in Huerta: Los Cuatro Bolos, "The Four Cakes." At 11:30 p.m., we came back, cleaned the flat, and packed.

An interesting thing happened today. There was a terrorist attack in Burgos (we were there just a few days ago, about an hour away), but I guess no one was killed, so that is good. We are leaving tomorrow morning—hopefully we'll get to the airport in time!! But, I still do not know what Phoebe wrote in her letter. I wonder when I will know and why this anxiety is so difficult to bear!

Chapter 11

Back Home in Indiana—August, 2009

From: Phoebe, your servant in the Church of Jesus Christ here in Rome

To: Paul, my beloved brother and esteemed apostle of the Lord Jesus Christ

Spring, the tenth year of the reign of Emperor Nero

May the grace and peace of the Lord Jesus be yours today and always. You know how I love you in the Lord Jesus and how much you mean to me—someone who has not known love in the traditional sense. Your • treatise on love in the letter to the church at Corinth when I was there, I took as written for me and so appreciate your kind concern.

The vow you took in Cenchrea, at my insistence, made me love you even more. I felt you had undervalued your Jewish heritage (and rightly so), but since you were returning to Jerusalem and had suffered some criticism from the Jewish community in Corinth, I pled with you to do something that would show your Pharisaic training had not been forgotten. On the other hand, the objective of your vow, to remain unmarried, disappointed me, as you know, but since your vow was for a relatively short time, I still had hope that you would return. You did, of course, but not before I had to go to Rome, due to the death of Urbanus, Father's business partner, at which time I carried your letter to the emerging church there.

When you arrived here in Rome a few years later, you asked me to write the story of God's marvelous work in my life since Dr. Luke had returned to Jerusalem, and no one was writing the account of your ministry and travels. I yearn to fulfill your every request.

As I shared with you in confidence while you were with me in Cenchrea, my given name is Salome Phoebe, daughter of Herodius and Herod Philip I. Father was not given a rulership portion because his mother Mariamne fell out of favor with Herod the Great. Named after Queen Salome Alexandra, Queen of Judea some three hundred years before I was born, and after Phoebe, the Greek mythological Titaness, I relished my education in the finest schools of art and science in Rome. When I was only fifteen, my mother eloped with my uncle, Herod Antipas, who came to Rome and lured her to Judea, where he had recently completed the construction of a beautiful new palace in the mountains overlooking the east shore of the Dead Sea called Machaerus.

Slapping all Jewish tradition in the face, they married while both were still married to their other spouses. Not that we had ever been very committed to our adopted religion, but we were living among the most traditional of all Jewish Pharisees. John the Baptizer decried this sin—the flaunting of which he considered to be the most flagrant abuse of Jewish law and culture—with very strong words in messages to the crowds that followed him. Mother hated him for it. Stepfather (Uncle) Herod Antipas was rather amused by John, but, at Mother's insistence, Uncle Herod Antipas sent soldiers to arrest him under the pretense that Herod was offering the Machaerus palace as protection from the Jewish leadership.

At that time, I must confess that my passion was the arts, music, and dancing, and I became an accomplished singer and dancer and would perform whenever requested. So at Uncle Herod's birthday celebration, when he asked me to dance for all the important people of the region, I was pleased to perform. My sensuous gyrations enraptured Uncle Herod who had obviously had too much to drink. So after the dance he promised, with an oath, to give me whatever I wanted, even to half of the Kingdom. Mother immediately demanded I ask for the head of John the Baptizer on a plate.

Although I was not thoroughly aware of the impact of my involvement in the martyring of John the Baptist, I never danced again. It was not until Jesus was crucified that it hit me that I had participated in the murder of the forerunner of the Messiah. In the meantime, I disguised myself as an older woman and began to tag along with the crowds who were following

Jesus. In fact, I spent so much time with Jesus and his disciples that Mother began to rigidly control my activities. I did get the chance, however, due to the Passover celebration, to witness the crucifixion and on Sunday, to furnish and bring the spices to the garden tomb. Unfortunately, Mother did not allow me to savor the miraculous upper room and Temple courtyard occurrences and shortly thereafter sent me back to Rome where, in God's goodness, I learned the minutiae of Father's import-export business.

Four years later, Uncle Herod Philip's wife died childless. (He is sometimes called Philip II, the Tetrarch of Iturea.) Father gave me to him, on one of his frequent trips to Rome, with the idea that I could produce an heir for him. Herod Philip II also died within the year, leaving me a widow, but since he had no heir, I was awarded an inheritance of considerable wealth.

Following the Jewish tradition, Uncle Aristobulus offered to take me as his wife, but since he already had a wife named Salome and had three sons, I decided to take my inheritance and move to Achaia (Greece). I also decided to change the name I was known by, from Salome, meaning "Peace," since I had no peace, to Phoebe, meaning "Radiant," and to see what God would pour out on me.

I did not have to wait long, for Father also died and Urbanus, his business partner, in Rome, doing quite well, asked me to take over the office in Cenchrea, seaport for Corinth, across the bay from Athens.

The work kept me very busy as a wealthy widow, but I found time to organize a group interested in discussing the possibility that Jesus was the Messiah. The group expanded to the Synagogue in Corinth, as I owned the house next door, occupied by Titus Justus. When God sent you we were ready to accept Christ as Savior and start the church. It still amazes me how God had used me to prepare this group to be the church, as immature as it was.

We became dear friends, as I hosted you and your team for over two years. (Some of the brethren thought you took advantage of my generosity and complained that you were in the ministry only for material gain.) When you left, you sent Apollos and his team, who were so accepted by everyone that they did not need a sponsor, but I stood up for you even though your letters were discouraging to some in the church. (Even though Apollos was still a disciple of John's at the time of his arrest, I had never met him and thus, my true identity was not revealed.) Then you sent Timothy and Titus, both of whom were the gentle leadership the church needed, and they so appreciated the help I was able to provide.

Before you returned, you counseled me to move back to Rome to take over the business as well as help the struggling church. Then Urbanus also died, and I had to go back to Rome, so I carried your letter intended for the church there.

Meanwhile, the trouble in Jerusalem kept you in prison for some time, and then God allowed you to appeal to Rome for justice. We heard about your shipwreck in Malta, since the grain on the ship was intended for our warehouse. We also heard about your miraculous deliverance from harm and injury. So when you arrived in Italy I met you with the brethren at the Forum and discreetly rented a house for you to live in. I was overjoyed and thankful for your presence and ministry, but remembering the criticism in Corinth, we refrained from displaying our affection for one another. Even though your vow was over, you felt constrained to follow through and remain unmarried, which I heavy-heartedly understood because of the counsel you had given to the church at Corinth.

Finally, after Julius, the Centurion in charge, was relieved, I was able to use Father's business influence to gain your release, but only for you to travel to Spain. (The officials thought that if you went back to Jerusalem without a final judgment, there would be no end to the trouble the Jews would cause.) Further, you felt a strong calling of God to minister to the unreached there in Spain. I desperately wanted to go with you, but you wisely chose Urbanus and Rufus, both devout Christians and Roman citizens.

We agreed that my letter needs to be made public so that God would be glorified, but only at the proper time. When you return to Rome, maybe it can be made known. Dr. Luke will know who to send it to.

May the Lord richly bless your efforts there

in Spain and give all the saints there our love and assurance of our prayers.

All my love, your sister, Phoebe

"Deena, this letter is amazing! Who translated it for you?" Aylea asked after reading it, as soon as she arrived from Papua in mid-August.

"When I went over to IMU to see if my job was still available, I asked Professor Yoder if he would like to translate it for me. He said he would love to do it, and here it is!"

"It really does fill in some of the details that are not recorded in the New Testament accounts. What part intrigues you the most?"

"The part where Phoebe explained that, when she followed through with her mother's demands to have John's head cut off, the impact of that action resulted in her becoming a dedicated Christian. So some good did come from John's tragic death. I am assuming that her consecration and service were one of the reasons why God allowed John the Baptist to be beheaded. You know how that has bothered me for so long. But in some ways, for me the letter raised more questions than it answered. For instance, when she persuaded the judge to free Paul to go to Spain, was she unknowingly sending him to be set up for his death? Or did he, by his firm, unrelenting pursuit of converts, make enemies there? And what happened to the church that was planted in Clunia or the area nearby?"

"You remember that when Rome burned, Nero blamed the Christians," her mother mused. "It could be that all the colonies took up his depraved cause and considered Christians expendable, so they ruthlessly persecuted and killed them. But as you found out, there are churches all over Spain. Did the letter answer your questions about Apollos?"

"You're right, Mom, I need to reflect on the positive. I had an inkling that Apollos may have been in Judea about the time John was there baptizing, and this letter confirms that feeling."

"To change the subject, it looks like your job has been filled?"

"Yes, they found another needy freshman and gave the job to her."

"What are you going to do now?"

"Well, that's something I need to talk to you about. I've been in communication all year with my friends at Toccoa Falls College, and as sophomores, they are now moving into Paradise Mountain, the MK home, and say that they are sure the TFC scholarship offer and vacancy at Paradise Mountain are still available for me. So I've been praying about transferring there. What do you think?"

"I'll pray about that with you," Aylea smiled. "Back to the letter. What do you think about the vow Paul took in Cenchrea?"

"I have always felt that Luke had some reason for not explaining why Paul took the oath in such a dramatic fashion, other than it was a Jewish custom. So when Phoebe explained that she was the motive, I felt validated. Maybe it was merely that she felt that Paul should return to his Jewish roots for the trip. Or, maybe there were some romantic feelings between the two, but Paul was convinced that the Lord wanted him to remain single so he would suffer the persecution he would face without involving someone he loved and wanted to protect."

The annual mission conference of Sugar Ridge Church was planned for the coming weekend. Helen Werner, Bible translator from the Kayavani tribe in Brazil, was scheduled to be the main speaker Saturday evening. Helen, almost eighty, yet still spry and alert, enjoyed sharing her work of Bible translation in the Amazon jungle. Since the emphasis of the conference was Bible translation, Aylea and Carol were also asked to share about their work in Papua on the first evening, Friday. Because of this, Aylea and Deena did not have much time together, other than when Deena helped Aylea polish her PowerPoint presentation.

Carol and Aylea had participated in the mission conference at Sugar Ridge on several occasions over the past twenty-five years. Many of the members knew of the struggles and triumphs involved in completing the New Testament in a previously unwritten language, and in teaching the people to use it in worship and instruction. Since the Old Testament was almost ready for publication, Carol highlighted the steps undertaken in preparation for publication. She went on to respectfully discuss the important role of the translation team members, who were also the church leaders. Aylea also mentioned their work, serving as consultants for some of the newer programs, and the spiritual results among some language groups as they heard God's word in their language for the first time.

Many attending Friday evening were impressed with all God was doing in Papua and asked how they could be involved. This gave Carol and Aylea an opening to present special prayer requests, opportunities to give toward projects that needed funding, and ways in which the people could even come and fill short-term or long-term personnel needs.

During the coffee fellowship time after the service, Pastor Mac found Deena with some of the other college students. "Deena, Dr. Yoder called this week and asked if I had heard about your extraordinary adventure this summer in Spain. I knew you were in Spain working on an archaeological dig, but hadn't, of course, heard about anything extraordinary. So he tried to be calm when he told me about the letter you found in a grave with three skeletal remains. That's pretty exciting, isn't it?"

"Yes, very exciting. If it can be shown that the letter is genuine, there could be a radical shift in the thinking about where Paul died."

"And you found it?"

"Yes. Actually, I found the first skeletal remains in the grave. Then I was asked to work on other areas of the dig site and other team members finished cleaning off the dirt from the skeletons. After pictures were taken and every bone meticulously removed and marked, I asked if I could look below the bottom of the grave and immediately found this copper tube—actually, it was a flat piece of copper rolled into a tube and sealed. It had to be opened in a special laboratory."

"And inside was a document?"

"Yes, the document was of papyrus, tightly rolled up. It took the lab several days, while we waited on pins and needles, to process the papyrus so it could be unrolled without damaging the ink."

"They gave you a copy of the document which was written in Greek?"

"Yes, and since there was no one there available to translate it into English for us, I brought it home and Professor Yoder did a draft for me. Dr. Hernando Torres of the Spanish University was also having someone translate the document for them. The original document belongs to the university because they are in charge and sponsor the dig."

"May I read it?"

"Of course. I have it in my Bible, over here, and you may make a copy for yourself."

"Thank you. This is amazing, almost earthshaking, wouldn't you say?

"Yes, I would. But I also pray that God would be glorified through this discovery and that many would respond as the Holy Spirit uses this new evidence of His reality and faithfulness."

"Could we talk about this together at the Sunday morning service?"

"Yes, of course we can."

Saturday evening, when Pastor Mac was introducing a young couple who had been on a short-term mission trip to Roatan, Honduras, he mentioned a "special surprise interview" for the next morning and that no one would want to miss it. The couple who spent two weeks in the villages of Roatan shared how they visited homes of the very poor with the gospel and provided some physical help, such as bread, rice, sugar, and drinking water. They were well-received in the Roatan community, and the local Roatan sponsoring church had noticed a marked increase in attendance since the group helped make the ministry known.

Helen, vibrant with her passion for the Kayavani people and Bible translation, shared the results of placing God's Word in the heart language of the people—how it has transformed lives of whole villages and even groups of villages that speak the same language. At the end, she challenged the audience with this story:

"When Rose and I first entered the village as translators for the Kayavani speakers in the Amazon area of Brazil, we searched for someone who could help us with learning the language and then help us with Bible translation. We found a young Kayavani mother who was anxious to help and very talented in the language. As we were translating the gospel of Mark, this young Kayavani mother accepted the Lord as her Savior.

"After the gospel of Mark was published in Kayavani, the young mother held it up and asked, 'Your mother did not have this book, did she?'

"You might be able to tell from my accent that I am from Germany, and we, like those of you in the United States and United Kingdom, have had God's word in our language for centuries. 'Yes,' I confessed, 'my mother had this book.'

"Then she asked, 'Your grandmother did not have this book, did she?'

"'Yes,' I confessed again, 'my grandmother had this book.'

"Then this young mother shared with me what was on her heart. 'When I was a little girl, my grandmother told me that someone was going to come and tell us how to be free from sin and fear. Why didn't someone come and tell my grandmother?'

"Did God perhaps call a young man to go to the Kayavani people and share with this grandmother, whom He had prepared, how to receive the gospel, but the fellow said 'No'? When God speaks, it is vitally important to listen and obey. Let me challenge you here tonight. If God is speaking to you, please, please, wholeheartedly accept His call and obey. I can promise you: You will never be sorry!" •

As Helen encouraged those whom God was calling to obey and become a part of what God was doing in the world, Deena noticed that her friend, Rachel Steinbeck, across the aisle, was sobbing uncontrollably. She got up and sat beside her. "Rachel, is something wrong?"

Rachel nodded. "That was Jack and me! I'll tell you later," she whispered between sobs.

Pastor Mac invited those whom God was calling to serve Him on the mission field to indicate their obedience by raising their hands. Several did, and he prayed that God would provide leading, training, funding, and peace. And he prayed that each one would daily renew their dedication to missions and realize their place in God's worldwide evangelization effort. Then the church was dismissed to the fellowship hall for refreshments.

Rachel took Deena by the hand and led her down the aisle to Helen, standing in the front of the church. Tearfully she stammered, "That was me, me and Jack!"

"What do you mean?" asked Helen.

Rachel regained control of herself. "That last story you told. My friend Jack and I dedicated our lives to go to the Kayavani people back in 1941, and then we did not go. But, praise God, you did go about twenty-five years later."

"Tell me, why did you not go?" Helen asked. At that moment Aylea joined them.

"I'm ashamed, but I was only sixteen and Jack eighteen. Daddy would not let us see each other anymore, but I'm sure it was really because he did not want me to go to Brazil."

"Why didn't Jack go by himself?"

"He was Daddy's farmhand, and when Dad sent him away, he joined the Navy. I suspect that he did it out of spite because we are pacifists. Jack died in the bombing of Pearl Harbor by the Japanese."

They were all quiet for a moment, then Aylea said tremulously, "You may wonder why God allowed all this, but I believe that this was part of God's permissive will. As you may know, I'm Japanese and my uncle, Mitsuo Fuchida, led the attack on Pearl Harbor. You may also know that Jake DeShazer, who bombed Japan with Doolittle's Raiders, was captured and held prisoner. And that he found Christ in a Japanese prison. After the war, he returned to Japan as a missionary, led my uncle to the Lord, started a church in my hometown—the town he had bombed—led me to the Lord, and challenged me to be a missionary in Papua. There Deena was given to me as an orphan. And, now, she has learned that, even in the most devastating experiences, God can produce good or even life-changing results, for eternity, in people's hearts! I am also aware that Rachel here has multiplied herself over and over with the young people she has challenged to serve the Lord as missionaries."

Deena pulled the other three ladies close to her, and with their arms around each other she prayed: "Dear Lord, we are all amazed and overwhelmed with Your goodness, Your leading, Your sovereignty, and Your provision. I pray for Your servant, Rachel, who needs Your peace and Your wisdom, to embrace Your permissive will in each of our lives and in the world. I thank You for Helen, who has faithfully served for decades, and saw You work in many people groups for Your honor and glory. I thank You for my mom, who loves me and showed me Your love, patiently answering my questions when she could, and, together, seeing Your hand for the 'rest of the story.' Be glorified in us right now!"

Sunday, August 23, 2009

Sunday morning, at church, Deena, looking radiant in her new black sundress accented with a colorful bead necklace from the market in Burgos, Spain, and black high-heeled sandals, was called to the front to help the worship team sing the last song before the sermon. It was her favorite: "I've Got a River of Life". They led the congregation, singing:

> I've got a river of life flowing out of me,
> Makes the lame to walk and the blind to see;
> Opens prison doors, sets the captives free,
> I've got a river of life flowing out of me.
> Spring up, O well, within my soul!
> Spring up, O well, and make me whole
> Spring up, O well, and give to me
> That life abundantly.

After the prayer, Pastor Mac asked Deena to bring her microphone and come to the pulpit. "Most of you know Deena Fuchida. She has been attending here a year and is a student at IMU. Deena, tell the congregation what you have been doing this summer."

"I had the distinct privilege to participate in an archaeological dig in Clunia, Spain. Clunia was a Roman colony founded about 100 BC and abandoned about AD 400. It has just been in recent years that archaeologists have endeavored to dig up and preserve the remains of the city. This year our team was unearthing part of the amphitheater, probably the largest in Europe."

"What did you find there?"

"Amazing as it may seem, we found many artifacts that can be dated as early as the first century AD. As we were digging just outside the platform or the stage area of the amphitheater, we found graves, places where people had been buried. I personally found one grave that held the skeletal remains of three people."

"What did you find under the bones?"

"I found a copper tube. Copper was available in Jesus' day and was even used to copy Scripture onto. But this tube was sealed. We sent it to a special laboratory where it was opened up. Inside, they found a document written on papyrus. It took the lab over a week to process the rolled up papyrus such that it could be unrolled without too much damage to the ink on the papyrus."

"Before you left, did the lab get it unrolled?"

"Yes, and it was a letter from Phoebe to the apostle Paul. You remember Paul commended Phoebe to the Roman Church in Romans 16." All eyes were on Deena; not a sound could be heard throughout the congregation.

"Did you get a copy and have it translated into English?"

"Yes, and I have it here. Shall I read it?"

"Please do!"

After Deena read the letter, Pastor Mac let her go back to her seat. Then he told the story of Rachel, Jack, Helen, Aylea, and Deena, emphasizing God's sovereignty and love. He shared the plan of salvation and gave an invitation. As Deena prayed in her pew, she realized that several people were responding by going forward and kneeling at the altar. She prayed that those going for salvation would have a life-changing experience, and that those going forward to dedicate themselves to missionary service and God's plan for their lives would be completely dedicated to Him and His will. When she finally looked up, she was completely surprised to see two people she knew, but never expected to see at the altar—Sharon and Rick. She hurried down the aisle and knelt beside Sharon. She listened as Sharon prayed out loud, asking God to forgive and come into her life. With tears she repeated the prayer the counselor suggested she pray and then she looked up smiling and said, "Something has happened to me. I feel free and completely clean! I feel like I'm floating on air!"

Deena prayed, "Thank you, Jesus. Thank you, Jesus."

In a few moments, Rick also lifted his head and smiled, saying, "I don't understand it, but it's better than any high I've ever experienced! I believe God is taking away my need for alcohol and drugs!"

Looking at Deena he exclaimed, "Did you hear that, Deena? Your prayers have been answered! I'm singing "I've Got a River of Life". Do you know, now, why you went to Clunia? Not only to find Phoebe's letter, but to help me find God!"

Pastor Mac came over, and Deena introduced them.

"Rick, if you are from Ohio State and Sharon is from Loyola of Chicago, how did you get together here?"

Rick motioned for Sharon to answer. "It's been about three weeks since we left Clunia. Rick and I have kept in contact because we felt we needed what Deena has, a close relationship with God. Finally, we decided to meet here and ask Deena what we needed to do. I am three hours away and Rick about four. Knowing Deena would be at church this morning, we thought we would leave home early and come and surprise her. I called and found out the Sunday morning service was at 10:30, so we decided to meet in front of the church about that time. I arrived a little early and Rick a few minutes late, so we had no time to find you, Deena, before the service. We were shocked to see you in such an important role, but we learned that God is in charge, and then, Pastor, you told us exactly what we wanted to know, and guess what? We found it!"

Just someone else interrupted, "Deena, will you introduce me also?"

She turned. It was James. She greeted him enthusiastically with a hug. "What are you doing here?"

"I came to see you! You invited me, remember?"

"This is my friend from Papua, James Park—Pastor Mac, Sharon, and Rick. These two were both with me in Spain. I guess you know that from our e-mail and Facebook messages."

James grinned. "Yes, and we've been praying for both of you. God answered our prayer!"

Epilogue

Baliem River Bank—June, 2012

"I've always imagined that the Baliem dances its way from the high mountains to the south coast," exclaimed Deena as she and James reached the park area near Wamena for a picnic. "But the dances change as the river descends. Here it waltzes around Wamena, don't you think?"

"Well," James responded, "I think it waltzes across the south lowland, appearing to be almost stopped, but with a lot of water quietly twisting and turning to the coast. Here, I think it is somewhat faster, maybe like a schottische, slower than a foxtrot, but still moving incessantly. Maybe it tangos. What do you think?"

"You're right, as usual." Deena smiled. "Thank you for arranging to spend our honeymoon at home in Papua. This is so beautiful, and I am so happy!"

James had proposed marriage to Deena in December 2011, when they both were back in Papua for Christmas. Their wedding, held at First Church, Toccoa, was celebrated the Saturday after finals so all their friends from college could attend. Everyone was delighted, saying how beautiful and God-honoring it seemed.

It was, however, the Christmas before, back in Papua, where

God opened the door for them to return to the place where they had grown up and called home, as missionaries. James, studying summers, had graduated in May of 2011 in cross-cultural studies and then went on for his master's degree while Deena finished her BA, also in cross-cultural studies.

James's specialty for his master's program was cross-cultural community development, and his master's project was to plan a training program that could be held in the villages of interior Papua at the request of the local village leadership. While they were in Papua in December of 2011, James proposed the idea to the directors of the Evangelical Church. They enthusiastically approved the proposal and invited James and Deena to return and initiate the program based on the following requirements:

Name: *Hari Baru—Pendidikan Tanpa Perbatasan* (New Day—Training without Boundaries)

Vision: Train emerging church leaders on-site to meet the local, district, national, and worldwide criteria.

Method: Local pastors and leaders to identify training needs, participants, and the week-long training dates. Selected HCA students to mentor young trainees and learn from the experience. Selected church leaders to monitor, guide, and learn for their future programs.

Core Courses:
- Scriptures
- Literacy—vernacular and national language
- Health, hygiene, and sanitary practices
- Heritage and history
- Cultures and geography

Practical Application:
- Agriculture
- Business
- Music
- Worship
- Computers
- Sewing

"I know I shouldn't be—but I am so nervous about next week when we initiate our first program in my own village."

"You're right this time, Deena: you should not be nervous," her husband smiled. "But it is sometimes more difficult to return home where people remember you as you were, and you know it! Your relatives love you and are excited about what God is going to do through our efforts. We are merely participants in His elaboration of the rest of the story."

Made in the USA
Lexington, KY
03 December 2014